Not Waving

For Thomas and Charlotte

NOT WAVING

Sarah Grazebrook

Hutchinson
London Melbourne Auckland Johannesburg

This edition first published in 1987 by Hutchinson Ltd, an imprint of
Century Hutchinson Ltd, Brookmount House, 62–65 Chandos Place,
London WC2N 4NW

Century Hutchinson Australia Pty Ltd.,
PO Box 496, 16–22 Church Street, Hawthorn, Victoria 3122, Australia

Century Hutchinson New Zealand Limited,
PO Box 40–086, Glenfield, Auckland 10, New Zealand

Century Hutchinson South Africa (Pty) Ltd.,
PO Box 337, Bergvlei, 2012 South Africa

Set in $^{11}/_{13}$pt Sabon by
Input Typesetting Ltd, London
Printed and bound in Great Britain by
Anchor Brendon Ltd, Tiptree, Essex.

British Library Cataloguing in Publication Data

Grazebrook, Sarah
    Not waving.
    I. Title
    823′914[F]   PR6057.R33/

ISBN 0–09–168110–3

'Oh, no no no, it was too cold always
(Still the dead one lay moaning)
I was much too far out all my life
And not waving but drowning.'
                    Stevie Smith

'This is nice,' said Delia. 'Is it M and S?'

'Yes,' lied Ginny, casting a doleful eye at the leeks protruding from the pedal bin.

'But anyway, I do think we should all go.'

Ginny tried to look non-committal.

'So shall I pick you up? Or will you make your own way? Actually, come to think of it, you could bring Sally. That wouldn't be too much of a bind, would it? She could come with me or Madeleine otherwise. What do you think? Perhaps it would be better if Madeleine brought her. Then we'd be sure she got there all right.'

Ginny wanted to say she hadn't crashed for a fortnight, but found herself murmuring, 'Honestly, Delia, I don't think. . .'

'Oh, don't worry about Raymond. He won't object. Probably be quite chuffed. I don't suppose you could get him to come along, could you? Richard's coming, and Martin Banks might – I'm quite surprised about him, really. Not the supportive type, I'd've said. Still, you never know.'

Ginny got up to fetch the salad.

'Vari's coming,' Delia added. 'She's bringing the twins.'

'I thought they had bottles.'

'They do, but who's to know?'

'They might.'

'If I were you, I'd come by tube. Oh. Endive.'

'You don't like it?'

'Yes, I do. Usually. Oh, Ginny, you're not drinking plonk, are you? What will Lizzie make of it?'

'I don't think she minds. Anyway, she's more or less weaned. That's why I don't think I'm really qualified. . .'

'Of course you are. No one's going to notice if there's anything coming out.'

'Lizzie will.'

The phone rang. It was Mitchell. Ginny tried to sound casual.

'Yes. Wednesday.'

Delia was peeling a pear.

'Are these from the garden?'

'Yes.'

'How's Matthew?'

'He's very well.'

'He always looks so thin.'

'Yes.'

'Why is that, do you suppose?'

'I suppose it's because he's so thin.'

'Do you feed him?'

'Not much.'

'You should, you know.'

'Yes. I'll make some coffee.'

'Oh, not for me.'

'Tea?'

'Have you any camomile?'

'I expect so.'

'Lovely.'

Mitchell kissed the inside of her fingers.

He was very worried about Ginny. She was a disgrace to his class. Her head was never underwater.

'He'll never do it, if you don't.'

'I know that. Of course I know it. I keep trying.'

'Are you worried about your hair?'

'Why, will it fall out?'

'No, but it might get messed up. Is that what worries you?'

Ginny kissed Mitchell's solicitous eyes.

'What worries me is that I might drown.'

'I won't let you drown.'

'I know you won't, but I might anyway.'

'How?'

'I'll tell you how afterwards.'

'I think you're being stubborn. How can I teach Matthew if he can see you're frightened of water? I can't say "Even Mummy can do it" if you can't.'

'I realise that. I am trying. I practise all the time.'

'Where?'

'In the bath. In the rain. Talking to Raymond's brother.'

'Eileen can do it.'

'So you keep telling me.'

'Eileen's a very good swimmer.'

'Is that why you married her?'

'I think so. She's very good at netball, too.'

'What a lot we must have in common.'

'It won't spoil your hair. Honest.'

'It won't improve my netball, either.'

Mitchell touched her ear.

'I don't like Mummy's toast.'

'Yes, you do. What's wrong with it?' Raymond Jeavons crunched his squelching Sunblest.

Matthew regarded his charcoal crescent bitterly. 'It's black.'

'That's because it's brown. Much better for you.'

'Why don't you have Mummy's toast, Daddy?'

'Because I'm grown up.'

'Mummy eats it. Isn't Mummy grown up?'

'Well, yes, she is.' Raymond thrashed around for an answer. 'But she's a lady.'

'Will I be a lady when I'm grown up?'

'Eat your breakfast.'

'I don't like it.'

'Matthew, I'm getting annoyed, and you know what that means. . .'

'Why can't I have some of yours?'

'I've eaten it.'

'It's not fair.' Matthew's spluttering anguish roused Ginny from her Sainsbury's list.

'What's the matter, darling?'

'It's not fair.'

'Well, nothing ever is, darling. I wouldn't cry about it.'

'I want Daddy's toast.'

'Doesn't Daddy want it?'

'He's eaten it all up.'

'What a good Daddy. Here, you can have a piece of mine.'

As Matthew thumped despairingly from the room, Ginny was vaguely aware that she had not helped.

'That child's spoilt,' decreed Raymond.

'Is he?'

'Well, isn't he?'

'Yes.'

Ginny caught sight of Lizzie's upholstered bottom bustling into the larder, but was too late to prevent her feeding a sock through the Marmite.

'Are you home tonight?' she called from under the meat safe.

'Yes, I think so. Not before eight. I suppose you'll be in bed?'

'Probably.'

'Right. I'll have dinner with Matthew.'

'Actually, I'm meant to go to Delia's if you're in.'

'Again?'

'Yes. She wants to coordinate strategy for Wednesday. You remember, Raymond. It's the breast-feeding sit-in at Harrods.'

'What's that got to do with you?'

'She wants me to go.'

'Say "No".'

'I have.'

'So?'

'You know Delia.'

'But you're not even feeding Lizzie now. I'd be as much use as you. I've got a bigger chest.'

'Actually, Delia was rather hoping you might find the time.'

'Ginny, I'm not in favour of this. You know what that . . . Aaaaargh.' Raymond struggled ineffectually to prise Lizzie's tooth from his ankle.

'This child's worse than Jodhpur.'

'Only because she's alive.'

'Jodhpur was very gentle towards the end.'

'The end was a long time coming.'

Matthew, wearing Raymond's cummerbund and a cardboard box, snarled through Ginny's legs, 'I'm Jodhpur. Ruff ruff.'

'You'll be joining him if you're not careful.'

'Why's Lizzie got Daddy's fenoculars?'

'Because. . . What? Oh, Lizzie, darling. *Thank* you. Give them to Mummy. *Thank* you. Good girl.'

'I don't think you should go on this Harrods do. I don't much like the idea of my wife baring her all in front of total strangers.'

'What about Crete?'

'You were younger then.'

Raymond flounced down the hall, and out into the heady Acton air. He sensed a meagre victory.

Ginny carted the Habitat mugs to the sink and swilled them in the foamless water. Then she retrieved Lizzie from the sideboard where Matthew had succeeded in hoisting her, before hiding himself in the curtains, and unglued his Shreddies from the percolator. After that she went upstairs and stood naked on the edge of the bath, peering dejectedly at herself in the Mothercare cabinet, to see if Raymond was right.

Mitchell loved her body, but that, as he fondly reiterated, was because she was 'an older woman'. Older than what? Older than Eileen. Older than Mitchell. Older than Raymond, even. How could anyone be older than Raymond? Raymond had been born forty-four. His mother was younger than he was.

Alice, Raymond's mother, liked Ginny. She didn't know why. Unless it was because she'd married Raymond. She much preferred her to Eric's wife, Rosie, who was infinitely more hospitable and had a warm, stylish house on the Peterborough Estate, which could be reached on the District Line with only one change.

Ginny and Raymond's house was cold and scruffy, with odd Victorian posters advocating cures for sour belchings and scrofula, and with nowhere to sit. Newspapers clung to every corner, rustling with pique if you tried to evict them from the ill-matched kitchen chairs or prod them away from your sandwiches. Where the papers stopped, the plants began, dangling wistfully from shelves too high to dust and too low to ignore. Ginny failed to water them with dogged regularity. Alice would watch them, on her fortnightly visits, fade from vibrant spikiness to limp apologies for foliage. They reminded her of herself after an afternoon at the Red Cross.

'What does Raymond think about it?' asked Alice.

'He's rather cross,' said Ginny.

'You'll go, then?'

'I don't know, Alice. I can't say I want to, but Delia's so. . .'

'Pushy,' said Alice, splattering her coffee on to a colour supplement. 'I must say, if I were planning to tear my clothes off in public, I'd choose somewhere sunnier than Harrods. Why don't you all go over to Battersea? You could get the 49 from South Kensington.'

'You're missing the point. The protest is because a woman was turned out of the restaurant in Harrods for breastfeeding her baby.'

'Quite right, too.'

'Oh, Alice, you're so positive. I do envy you.'

'I can afford to be positive. No one's going to ask me.'

'That's the trouble. I'm quite convinced in my own mind that the whole thing's loony, but I haven't got the guts to tell Delia.'

'Do you want me to have the children?'

'Yes please.'

That Lizzie was a prerequisite for the demonstration was not mentioned.

Ginny spent the afternoon with Mitchell, who had hurt his knee umpiring a netball match.

Raymond sat by the baked potatoes in the Ploughboy's Arms, sipping his Guinness. He was trying to decide whether to take Ginny to Normandy with him, which would entail asking Alice to look after the children for a week.

Matthew would be all right, but what about Lizzie? She was notoriously temperamental – not above summoning the NSPCC if denied a second rusk. Anyway, perhaps Ginny wouldn't want to leave them.

Should he take them as well?

He quailed at the prospect.

He really should see more of the children. Come to think of it, he should see more of Ginny.

Ginny had changed. She was just as exasperating as ever, but she seemed to have stopped trying. If she forgot to fetch his suit from the cleaners, she would say, 'I can do it tomorrow,' which really wasn't the point.

Maybe she needed a break. He would take her. It would be just like old times. So long as she'd remembered to get his shoes heeled, and paid that blasted library fine.

Roebuck joined him. 'You look a bit down, Biggles. What's the matter? Ginny decided to come on the Normandy binge?'

Raymond shifted in his seat. 'Oh, no,' he said. 'No, she's not coming. Doesn't want to leave the kids.'

'Doesn't sound like Ginny.'

Raymond frowned. 'No, it's this project schedule for the RPs. Just wondering if I can get it off before we go.'

'Tell you what,' said Roebuck. 'I'm taking Helen along for the experience. Helen Craig from the pool. Bright girl. If you like I'll lend her to you for an afternoon when we get over there. That way you won't have to rush it through. Less chance of an error.'

'Thanks,' said Raymond. 'Same again?'

'Where are you this afternoon?' Mitchell asked.

'Breast-feeding Lizzie in Harrods.'

'Do you shop at Harrods?'

'Of course not. Except for birthday cards.'

'I don't like women flaunting themselves in public.'

'Well, it's not really flaunting. . .'

'Baring their bosoms in public. It's not feminine.' He undid her blouse and gently cupped his hand round her breast.

'Anyway, no one'd notice yours.'

'Flatterer,' said Ginny, curling in to him. Later Mitchell told her that Eileen was at the fertility clinic.

'She really wants a baby, you know. She gets in such a state. She thinks it's her, you see. She won't even play in the team now. She thinks it's upsetting her cycle. All that jumping around.'

'Doesn't she jump around with you?'

Mitchell looked at Ginny reproachfully and made her feel cheap.

'I keep saying to her "Look, it might be me. Why don't we both see the doctor?" She won't hear of it.'

'Why not?'

'She thinks it means I'm queer if I can't give her a baby.'

'Who told her that?'

'Her mam, I expect.'

'Shall I write you a reference?'

Mitchell smiled and they made love again, but without much joy.

Eileen didn't like Dr Christian. He talked over the top of his half-moon glasses and grunted at her replies before referring back to her notes, as though checking the veracity of her words.

'Ummm, I can't help feeling, Mrs Mitchell, that you're worrying yourself unnecessarily. You're a young, healthy woman and you've only been married' – he consulted the card – 'just over two years. . .'

'Nearly three,' Eileen corrected.

Dr Christian lowered his eyes then nodded.

'Three years is not such a very long time, Mrs Mitchell. Ummm, have you been trying for a child ever since you were married?'

Eileen looked perplexed.

'Ummm, did you practise any form of contraception after your marriage?'

'I was on the pill.'

'For how long?'

'About a year.'

'Ah yes. So in fact you've only been trying to conceive for just over a year?'

'Nearly two.'

'Umm, what is your husband's attitude?'

'What to?'

'Towards having a child.'

'He wants one.'

'Are you certain of that? You've discussed it with him?'

'Course I have. I wouldn't be here otherwise, would I? He said I should come because it was getting him down. Me being so moody and that.'

'Umm, so you're moody?'

'Well, wouldn't you be? All my sisters've got kids.

Jeanette's got two, and Marion's just had a boy, and she's only been married six months. And she's younger than me.'

'You see, Mrs Mitchell, it's quite possible that the strain of wanting a baby is causing emotional stress in your relationship with your husband. And this could, umm, shall we say, interfere with the natural flow of things.'

'That's what I want, isn't it? If my natural flow would just stop for a bit I'd be all right, wouldn't I?'

Mitchell was watching the six o'clock news when Eileen got in. He had a mug of tea and a copy of *The Warden* open on his lap. He looked up as she came past to hang up her coat.

'How'd it go?'

'I dunno.'

'What happened?'

'Nothing happened. This twit asks me a load of rubbishy questions, then a nurse weighs me and gives me all these bloody leaflets. I could cry, honest.'

She slumped downn at the table and began to. Mitchell put his mug and book carefully on the chair arm and stood over her, shoulders hunched in silent condolence. Gently he put his fingers on the back of her neck and rubbed it soothingly. 'It'll be all right. There's nothing wrong with you. More likely to be me than you.'

'Oh, shut up,' screamed Eileen and stormed from the room.

Mitchell heard her thump on to the bed. The sobs came rhythmically. Muffled by the ceiling, they had an almost soporific quality. For a while he listened sorrowfully, but gradually, as they showed no sign of gaining in strength or decreasing in volume, he let his eyes, and hence his thoughts, return to the television.

'You're not cold, are you?' asked Ginny, hurling open the kitchen window to allow the north wind in.

Alice shrank behind the corner of the dresser. 'No, dear,' she shuddered. 'I'll just fetch my cardigan.'

'Say if it's too much,' her daughter-in-law admonished. 'It gets so stuffy in here when the sun's out.'

Alice knew from experience that anything much above freezing meant 'stuffy' to Ginny. Anything below was merely 'close'. For someone so at odds with nature in the garden, it seemed strange that she should welcome the elements into her own home quite so enthusiastically. Victorian houses on the whole are not remarkable for their cosiness, but Ginny had rendered her own centrally heated abode a test area for thermal underwear among her general acquaintance. No radiator ever crept to its full capacity without being twitched down to medium or worse. Only the children survived in relative warmth, due to their rooms being in the extension which had a flat roof, and a consequent tendency to get 'parky'.

Raymond objected with understandable vehemence to a house lined with tepid iron ware. 'What's the point of paying for fifteen bloody radiators if they're never on?' he would moan, running his fingers along the chilly metal.

'It's more economical,' Ginny would assure him right-eously. 'Gas has gone up again.'

'It would be more economical to live in a tent on the common,' was Raymond's plaintive rejoinder, 'and probably a lot warmer.'

Ginny forbore from suggesting he try it, but while he was in the cellar looking for claret, her fingers would deftly readjust the thermostat to a more personally acceptable level.

After a time Raymond got used to it, but Alice never had.

'Matthew ate all his tea,' she said to take her mind off her approaching hypothermia.

'Oh, good boy. What did you have?'

'Crisps,' said Matthew.

'Was that all?'

'And a last night.'

For reasons best known to himself, Matthew always referred to chocolate biscuits as 'last nights'.

'A good square meal,' said Ginny reprovingly, and tottered into the hall. She had had two gins at her friend Emma's on the way home. 'Is Lizzie in bed?'

'Yes,' said Alice, 'but she hasn't had her tea yet. She was so tired when we got in, I put her down for a snooze.'

'When was that?' groaned Ginny.

'About five o'clock.'

Lizzie would dance till dawn. 'Thanks for having them. Have you got a drink?'

'Of course. Raymond rang. He'll be in about nine.'

'Oh?'

'He's playing squash with Desmond.'

'What in, I wonder?' mused Ginny, casting a resigned glance at his kit underneath the breakfast bar. 'Are you staying to supper?'

'No, thanks. I've got some kidneys.'

'Oh, Alice, don't poison yourself again.'

'Of course I won't. They've hardly passed their sell-by date.'

'How long is hardly?'

'Four days. Maybe five. When was the fourteenth?'

'It's the twenty-fifth today. Why don't you stay? I'm going to do a bolognese.'

'No, really, Ginny. I can't. I've a thousand things to do. Shouldn't be here now, if the truth were known.'

'Well, have another drink.'

'All right. Just one.'

Eileen was angry.

She sat in front of 'Crossroads', arms clamped uncomfortably across her ample bosom, shoulders stiff with resentment, her upper lip jutting defiantly at no one.

Mitchell was making a curry. Devotee of Madhur Jaffrey, he chopped and chivvied, sliced and pounded, 'My Music' buzzing softly at his elbow. With mounting fury, Eileen watched him set the cutlery back to front and forget the serving spoons, as usual. She didn't move her handbag. Finally she stalked upstairs and stayed there for ten minutes, so that the poppadoms would go soggy.

Serenely she descended. Mitchell was reading his book. He got up.

'Ready to eat?'

'I suppose so.'

He served the food. Eileen picked at the rice and gnawed at her chapati fretfully.

'Did they say anything else?'

'Who?'

'The clinic.'

'Not really.'

'Well, what did they say?'

'Nothing.'

'They must've said something.'

'I can't remember.'

'Do you have to go back?'

Eileen nodded.

'When?'

'I don't know. Not for months. The card's there somewhere.'

'Can I look?'

Eileen shrugged. Mitchell flipped through the luncheon

vouchers and cleaning tickets, extracting a puce St Joseph's card.

'Not till November.'

Eileen snapped at a poppadom.

'They can't be over worried, then. What did they say?'

'I can't remember. Nothing much.'

'Oh, come on, love. For "nothing much" you're making a hell of a fuss.'

Eileen fairly spat at his insouciance. 'They said two years wasn't such a long time to be trying and just to keep at it.'

Mitchell's arm slithered around her. ' 'Appen they're reet, lass.' Eileen made to escape, but his hand had got too far and, one way or another, she found herself transported wholesale on to the real astrakhan rug in front of the SuperSer.

Mitchell made tea. 'I know what we'll do. We'll make a chart and stick it on the wall.'

'What sort of a chart?'

'A chart of how many tries we have, then next time you see the doctor you can show him and ask if we're trying hard enough.'

Eileen giggled, appalled.

Raymond came in at ten past nine, looking flushed and ebullient. Alice was stirring the spaghetti.

'Hullo, Mother. Still here?'

'I appear to be.'

'Did you win?' asked Ginny, handing him the bread board.

'More or less.'

'Which?' asked Alice.

'Des sprained his thumb in the second of three, so we abandoned the match.'

'Who won the first?'

'Really, Mother, does it matter?'

'I've always admired your faith in Things to Come.' Alice glided past him with the Parmesan cheese.

'Shall I open some wine?'

'I've done that,' said Ginny. 'It's breathing on the sideboard.'

'How d'you get on at Harrods?' he demanded of Ginny.

'Oh, all right.'

'What happened?'

Ginny, who had been briefed by Emma on the afternoon's events, shrugged vaguely. 'Not a lot.'

'Well, did you or didn't you?'

'Did I or didn't I what?'

'Bare your bloody tits in the restaurant?'

'No.'

'Aha,' her husband scoffed, 'I knew you wouldn't.'

'I thought you disapproved.'

'Not at all. I just knew you wouldn't have the nerve.'

'There were a lot of women who did.'

'They probably had something to show.'

'Probably.'

'How did you get out of it?'

'I said I couldn't afford a cream tea, and since there was such a queue it seemed a bit mean to take up one of the tables.'

'Typical Ginny. All talk and no do.'

Ginny broke off a piece of bread and coated it in butter. 'I did meet a photographer on the way out,' she told him between mouthfuls. 'He said he couldn't get a proper focus on thirty-five bosoms, so would I mind if he just photographed mine.' Raymond's wine came down his nose. 'From the neck down, of course,' Ginny smiled demurely.

After supper, Alice, having declined Raymond's blurred suggestion that he drive her to the tube, set off at scout's pace with Ginny in tow, for the Piccadilly Line.

'Promise you'll get a cab at the other end?'

'Of course I will. I always do.'

'Liar.'

'Well, it's not worth it for that distance.'

'You can be mugged on your own doorstep.'

'Precisely. I can hardly ask the man to drive straight through the french windows.'

'You know what I mean.'

'Darling, I know exactly what you mean. If it's any consolation to you there's a sixteen-year-old bobby who guards the Lobelia exit. He always sees me home.'

'You should've driven her,' Ginny accused.

'Whatever for?'

'Because it's late.'

'Precisely why I didn't want to. I'm worn out.'

'You should join the Samaritans.'

'She didn't have to stay. She comes to lunch and stays till eleven o'clock. What does she expect?'

'Nothing. From you.'

'You're not wearing that, are you?' Raymond frowned as Ginny came into the kitchen.

'What's wrong with it?'

'It's a bit . . . informal.'

'I'm an informal person.'

'Yes. Well, that's all very well amongst friends. . .'

'Emma and Peter are friends.'

'I know they are, Ginny, but you don't know who else is going to be there.'

'I'll lay forty to one it'll be Jane and Chris, Michael and Susie, Elaine and Patrice, and both sets of parents.'

'You know what I mean.'

'No, I don't.'

'I'm not going to argue about it. I just think you'd look better in something else.'

'Like purdah?'

'Oh, really, Ginny, if you're going to adopt that attitude. . .'

But Ginny had gone, slamming down the steps to the car. In her rage she had forgotten the linen jacket destined to cover what Raymond regarded as taboo. The dress itself was not immodest, but it was cream and the invitation said 'Drinks in the garden at 12'. Raymond followed his wife with a sinking heart. Ginny would be transparent!

'At least try to stay out of the sun,' he grunted gloomily as they walked up the path to Emma and Peter Bailey's Edwardian semi, where the party was buzzing cheerfully.

'Ginny . . . Raymond . . . Come in. Where are the kids?'

'At my mother's.'

Peter ushered them in as Raymond proffered the Côtes du Rhône. 'Thanks. Emma. . . It's Ginny and Raymond.'

Emma, Ginny's best friend, emerged with a tray of volau-vents, which she immediately handed to Raymond while she hugged his wife. 'What a gorgeous dress!' she exclaimed. 'Come out into the garden. It's boiling in here. Bring us a drink, would you, Peter? I must tell Ginny about Delia's latest project.' And they were gone, leaving the two men, who detested each other heartily, to cope with the canapés as best they might.

'What shall I do with these?' Raymond asked feebly.

'Would you mind passing them round while I just see to the drinks?' Peter backed away unhelpfully. Raymond considered this an unsuitable request but at least it gave him an excuse to stay indoors. If Ginny were hell-bent on making an exhibition of herself, as usual, he reflected morosely, the best thing for him would be to keep well away from her. Having so decided, he surveyed the room, and prepared to launch himself on the Jenkins' au pair, who spoke seven words of English but wore very short skirts.

Ginny and Emma sat on the low wall, toes dabbling in the fish pond. Someone had dropped a sausage roll into it and Ginny watched it slowly disintegrating, the pastry floating Ophelia-like amongst the pond weed, and the sausage upending against a stone like an unexploded torpedo. The sun was very hot.

'Well, well,' said a voice. 'Ducks are a-dabbling, uptails all.'

'Oh, hallo, James,' said Emma with scant enthusiasm. 'You know Ginny, don't you?'

'Raymond Jeavons' lovely wife, if I'm not mistaken,' James acceded. 'Mind if I join you?'

'There's not much room,' Emma pointed out, but her position as hostess debarred her from a more forceful protest.

James oozed in between them, knocking over Ginny's wine as he did so. 'Oops!' he beamed. The two women exchanged glances. James reached behind Emma and took a piece of quiche off Ginny's plate, which she had secreted in the shade of a currant bush to stop the salad cooking. 'Shouldn't leave it about if they don't want it eaten,' he sniggered as a slice of tomato tobogganed down his shirt front. It was only halted in its descent by the glistening paunch peeping grotesquely from between his shirt buttons.

At this point Emma disloyally abandoned her friend, promising to return with fresh drink, but since it was her party, she was inevitably waylaid en route for the kitchen, and Ginny last caught sight of her ushering a newly arrived couple towards the buffet on the verandah.

With the departure of Emma, Ginny nurtured the hope that James would at least move up a bit. It was a very small wall and a very hot day. James, however, showed no inclination to do so, and continued to chomp his way through her lunch with nauseating gusto.

'Is Sally with you?' she enquired, mainly to drown the noise of his chewing.

'She's over there somewhere.' James showered her with pastry. 'Feeding Alastair.'

Ginny tried to remember which of the two etiolated infants permanently clamped to Sally's breast was Alastair. 'How are the children?'

'Fine. Fine. Both got colds, of course.'

'Of course.' Ginny recalled that on the rare occasions when the boys had been seen to emerge from inside their mother's blouse, they had always had runny noses.

James bent down, and Ginny noted with dismay that he was untying his laces. Sure enough, a few more tugs and his bobbly toes were plopping about in the water beside her.

'What's that?' he squealed.

'It's a sausage,' said Ginny, 'someone dropped it in.'

'Bet I can reach it before you,' James chortled. 'Come on. You've got to do it with your feet.'

'Do what with your feet?' Ginny looked up. Emma was back. Silently she handed Ginny a glass of wine.

'I say, any chance of one for me?' asked James.

'Yes, of course. I'm sorry, I forgot you were over here. Peter's in the kitchen. Do go and help yourself.'

'That's all right. Ginny and I can share this one.'

'No, we can't.' Ginny struggled to her feet and began to grope her way across the grass.

'Sorry.' Someone had stood on her bare foot. Ginny grimaced. 'Why have you only got one shoe on?'

'It's a good way of meeting people.'

'How so?'

'You might never have spoken to me if you hadn't broken my toe first.'

'True. I must remember that in future.'

'It doesn't work in embassies.'

'You've tried it before?'

'I have it on good authority.'

'Ginny . . . Ginny . . . I've got something you want.'

Ginny's heart plummeted at the spectacle of bare-footed James hopping across the lawn, belly rippling rhythmically in the barely perceptible breeze.

'Is this your husband?'

'No, thank God. I'm trying to get away from him.'

'I can't say I blame you. By the way, I'm Richard, and this,' the bronzed Apollo drew a creature of bewitching beauty from the bunch of women discussing IUDs round the pâté, 'is Ilona.'

'Hullo,' said Ginny glumly, and, snatching her sandal from James's sweaty fingers, she hobbled into the house.

'Emma does know some boring people,' Raymond muttered to Ginny, as a leggy pharmacist made good her escape from the corner in which she had been pinned while subjected to his tales of stock-car racing in Wensleydale.

'Like us?'

'Speak for yourself.'

'I usually do.'

'Are you drinking gin?'

'A bit.'

'How much is a bit?'

'Every other one.'

'Christ, Ginny, you know what happened last time you mixed them.'

'Actually, I don't. *You* know, and Emma knows, and from what I have gathered, a great many other people, most of them complete strangers, know, but I don't remember a *thing*.'

Ginny glided bumpily in the direction of what she took to be her friends Janice and Edmond. They turned out to be an Australian couple called Larry and Dot, who sucked Ginny into their cluster and peppered her with questions about ancestral homes, capital gains tax and primogeniture.

Ginny explained that a semi on Acton Hill, though certainly preferable to a shack on Rottnest, was some way short of a family seat. On tax, she observed that those to whom much had been given should occasionally expect to have much taken away, and lastly, having replenished her gin, that the rights of sons to inherit over and above daughters only gave credence to the well-known fact that women would succeed on their own merits, whilst men invariably needed a hundred yards' start.

'I suppose,' leered Larry, 'that you're one of those females who think women are the superior sex?'

'Not at all,' slurred Ginny. 'You'd be inferior whatever sex you were.'

Emma, perceiving that her friend was two steps from shedding her sundress and challenging Larry to prove his credentials likewise, steered her crisply towards the kitchen, where a beaker of Gold Blend was attached to her gesticulating palms.

Helen Craig hoped the infatuation would prove short-lived. She had understood the terms of her trip to France with Roebuck, and had considered the pros slightly ahead of the cons. Roebuck was attractive, albeit in a 'rising young executive' way. He had hair, teeth, and played badminton. He also wore cotton shirts, which gave him a head start amongst potential JCV rivals.

On the boat over he had intimated that she would greatly oblige him if she could see her way to 'knocking out an hour's typing for old Biggles'. Somewhat aggrieved, she had acquiesced, and it was decided that Friday morning would be the most convenient for all concerned. Roebuck had a meeting in St Malo and would be away till dinner, so she would have the afternoon free to explore the old town.

Helen found Raymond boorish. His conversation was stilted, and he seemed to be making the minimum of effort to accommodate her inexperience as a secretary.

It was, she discovered, a markedly different affair taking direct dictation from the Head of Overseas Planning (Europe), to listening through headphones to Messrs Thorpe and Samson of Personnel. Her consequent nervousness manifested itself in a trickle of 'Pardon?'s, punctuated with flipping her hair from her forehead. This gesture lost more time, and altogether the business was progressing with painful slowness when Raymond chokily suggested that some fresh air might be helpful to them both.

Indecently relieved, Helen brushed aside the invisible lock and sat back in her chair.

Raymond got up and walked to the window. Placing both hands beneath the lower rim, he pushed. Nothing happened. He tried again. Still nothing. Raymond dusted his hands together and took a breath. Helen could see that he was exerting considerable pressure on the wooden frame. She could also see, from where she was sitting, that the frame was warped, and that the extraordinary force now being applied by the Head of Overseas Planning (Europe) was wrongly directed. If he didn't straighten up the sides it would never move.

What to do? The back of Raymond's ears had gone very pink and Helen suspected that his face was probably a good deal pinker. He had not, as yet, turned round. She dreaded the moment when he would. Raymond dreaded it even more.

One last try. There was an indefinable pop. One of his buttons had come off. 'Bugger,' said Raymond and swung round accusingly. Helen quailed. 'We'd better send for the porter. Order some coffee while we're at it, shall we?'

'That would be nice,' Helen murmured into her notepad.

'Yes,' agreed her senior and sat down again.

There was a pause. Raymond seemed to be consulting his notes. Helen feared he was about to renege on the suggestion, when he suddenly looked up, scrutinised her for a moment, and muttered, 'I don't suppose you speak the damn language, do you?' Overwhelmed, Helen burst out laughing.

'I do a bit,' she admitted, cheered by the knowledge that her three-month ordeal as an au pair in Nantes had not been entirely wasted.

'Right,' said Raymond purposefully, and rang for service.

'*Monsieur?*' The strawberry-marked Gallic beamed his eyes on Raymond and waited. Silence hung, crow-like, in the air, as Raymond went pink, cleared his throat, turned puce, coughed and flapped his hands frantically in Helen's direction.

'*Monsieur*' – she was on cue – '*s'il vous plaît, pourriez-vous nous ouvrir la fenêtre?*'

The man was obviously used to this request. Reaching behind the curtain, he withdrew a lengthy piece of timber and, with military precision, proceeded to batter the sides of the frame alternately until he judged them level. Replacing the wood, he positioned his hands under the frame and pressed. The window slid silkily upwards.

Raymond cleared his throat. The dreaded spectre of giggles hovered over Helen. Desperately she turned to the porter. '*Nous voudrions aussi deux tasses de café, s'il vous plaît.*'

'*Mais, bien sûr, ma'mselle. Tout de suite.*' He brushed his forehead in a manner reminiscent of Helen's own gesture and Raymond, for a moment, was struck with the thought that they were members of some Masonic lodge, bound, as they were, by this secret dialogue.

The man returned, bearing two thimbles of coffee and, for reasons best known to himself, a pat of butter. Helen thanked him warmly, whereupon he kissed her hand and pulled out several photographs. On closer inspection these were seen to be of his chickens, his car and his wife, seemingly in order of preference.

Raymond sensed that these confidences were in danger of lasting all morning, so he rose once more from his chair, walked to the window and tapped his watch significantly. Helen saw and understood. With a melting smile she gathered up the snaps and pressed them into the porter's hand. Still reiterating their gratitude, she edged him towards the door and, finally, through it, the two of them batting cries of '*Je vous en prie*' till he was well down the corridor.

This interlude bolstered Helen's confidence sufficiently to enable her to follow Raymond's grammarless outpourings without further difficulty. The dictation was concluded shortly before twelve, leaving her the typing, which she planned to dispatch before lunch, the afternoon then being free for exploration, and the evening for Roebuck.

Raymond, however, was also emboldened by the turn of events, and, delving deeply into his briefcase, murmured, 'Doing anything after lunch?'

Helen at first assumed he was talking to himself and continued checking her notes.

Raymond raised his eyes furtively. 'Any chance of a trip to the Musée d'Archéologie this afternoon?'

'Well, as a matter of fact. . .'

'Thought so. Never mind. Forget it.'

'I was thinking of going there myself.'

'Really? I don't suppose I could. . . You see, the thing is . . . I don't really . . . so it would be more than helpful if you could. . . Of course, if you prefer to go on your own. . .'

'It would be very nice to have someone with me,' said Helen. 'You know what the French are like.'

Raymond didn't know whether to feel elated or neutered. 'How long's this going to take?'

'About an hour.'

'Tell you what. . . Shall I give you a buzz about one? We could have lunch. I could do with some help with the damned menu anyway. Last night I had squirrel soup and chicken bones in custard.'

Helen smiled.

'Something like that, anyway. Agreed?'

'Certainly.'

For a moment Mitchell thought it was Ginny.

He thought right.

He was standing by the window of the diving pool, idly counting the bellyflops of an ageing oriental who was either made of leather or atoning for his failure to become a kamikaze pilot.

'Morning, Mr Mitchell.'

'Where's Matthew?'

'At school.'

'The little one?'

'She's gone to fight with Zoë.'

'Are you going in?'

'I'm going to have a sauna.'

'Ah. They're down the stairs on the right.'

'I know. I just thought I'd say hallo while I was here.'

'Good idea.'

'Perhaps we could have a cup of tea afterwards?'

'If I'm free.'

Ginny turned and made her way towards the ladies' sauna.

What a bloody stupid idea!

As she'd closed Emma's front door, the sound of Lizzie ramming the wall with her walker had filled her with a sense of helpless despondency. Nothing was ever going to change. There was she, thirty-seven-year-old mother of two, wife of a well-paid man in a dreary job. If it wasn't dreary, Raymond made it sound so. Trooping from coffee morning to bring-and-buy to 'just drinks and bits' with a feudal sense of duty that effectively obliterated the pleasure normally inherent in scandal and drunkenness.

She liked her children, she liked her friends, she certainly liked getting drunk. She didn't like it de rigueur.

But Ginny had Mitchell too. Mitchell made the rest bearable.

Mitchell, who only wanted her body and a small piece of her mind. The bit that mattered, where the dreams were. She would go and see Mitchell. So, they had agreed to stick to Wednesday lunchtimes and Friday after tea, with one Monday a month when Eileen had an away match. Not counting Matthew's swimming lessons, of course, when she would bob helplessly at the shallow end, trying to persuade her four-year-old to essay things she would rather die than attempt.

'Just hold your nose and touch the bottom darling. Pretend there's a lollipop stuck to it. No, I know there isn't really, but pretend.'

'Kick with your legs, Matthew. Both feet, that's right. Now count the stars. Lie back, kick, Oh, Christ. No, darling, I'm not doing it because I've got to hold Lizzie. Oh, hallo, Mr Mitchell.'

'Goodbye Mr Mitchell.'

He was obviously angry.

Perhaps he was part of the ritual, too. Wednesday, Friday, Wednesday, Friday, Wednesday, Friday, Monday, Wednesday, Friday. . . Or was she part of his? Perhaps there was someone else for Tuesdays and Thursdays, and Eileen for weekends? No wonder the poor girl couldn't get pregnant. He was probably worn out by Saturday.

'Mrs Jeavons.' Mitchell was standing by a door marked 'Staff'.

'Yes?'

'Could I see you for a moment?'

Ginny followed him through the swing doors. For a second she thought it was the sauna. Furious heat buffeted her from all directions, a desiccating, mothy warmth, hardly conducive to health and inner cleanliness.

The boiler room.

'In here.' Mitchell turned a key and stepped aside, as Ginny found herself in an oversized cubicle stacked high with cream and crimson towels, LBH etched challengingly round their borders.

Mitchell followed her in and shut the door. 'Now, Mrs Jeavons. . .'

He slung a pile of the gravelly linen on to the floor, dispersing them cheerily with his heels – rather like a bull preparing to charge, as Ginny reflected later.

'Mr Mitchell. . . No . . . someone might come in . . . Mitchell . . . *stop* it. . . What do you take me for?'

'A fucking good lay.'

They flopped into the sagging metal triangles foisted on the council by some over-persuasive designer. Ginny fidgeted around and finally gave up trying to make herself comfortable. 'You've hurt me,' she groaned.

Mitchell stirred his tea with a plastic spatula. 'You shouldn't have come.'

'I didn't,' said Ginny defensively. Mitchell laughed at the lie and Ginny giggled.

'Your spoon is melting.'

Mitchell's eyes reverted to his cup. 'Christ, it is too.' Mortified, he pursued the creamy globules fruitlessly round the beaker. 'I'm not drinking this.'

He rose and stalked purposefully to where Ivan, the token Pole, was dusting the sandwiches.

As he sat down again Ginny asked, 'Wouldn't he give you another?'

'He says it's Marvel.'

'And you believed him?'

'Well, the spoon's still here.'

'Yes, but look at it. It probably started off round.'

'That's evolution for you.' He grinned at her and she instinctively put out her hand to him but, of course, he didn't take it. Ginny felt the tears prickling her eyes.

'I'm going now,' she told him.

'Finish your tea.'

'I don't want it. You have it.'

'If you go now they'll think we're having it off.'
'What will they think if I stay?'
'They'll think we're having it off.'
Ginny stayed.
Later she asked Mitchell what he wanted most in the world.
'To train an Olympic diver.'
'And then?'
'Be kidnapped by Charlotte Rampling . . . Naked.'
'You or her?'
'Both of us.'
'Anything else?'
'Spend a weekend with you.'
'Where?'
'At your house. At my house.'
He wandered back to the side of the pool, and Ginny gathered her carrier bags and drove to Hammersmith, where she bought a lot of soap and some pork chops. Then she went home.

'Why don't you come?'

The girls sat in the dank changing room of St Etheldreda's Catholic Middle School. The match had been drawn, leaving both teams with a sense of unfinished business.

Susan Griffin, the goal attack, who had been at Farraday High with Eileen, peeled off her sweatband with such nicety that a stranger might have supposed her scalp attached to it. She was now intent on Pansticking her face with Warm Peach, a mistake in view of her newly auburned hair, and on persuading her friend to join her.

Eileen pulled off her plimsolls and considered the bruise erupting on the side of her knee.

'I don't think so. Thanks all the same, Sue. Another time.'

'You said that last time.'

'I know, but . . . you know . . . I ought to get back. I've got to get the tea.'

'Oh, come on, Eileen, your Dave can fry a couple of eggs for himself, can't he? I thought you said he was good at cooking.'

'He is. It's not that. . . It's just. . . You know.'

'No, I flippin' well don't. Honestly, Eileen, you're a right drag these days. It's only for a drink. My brother Gerry's over for a bit. You know, the one in the army. You'll like him. He's ever such a laugh.'

'I'm not sure. . .'

'Oh, go on. He's picking me up. He's got a fab car. It's an XR3.'

'I don't know. . .'

'Your Dave can come, too, if he wants.'

'He works late on Fridays.'

'There you are, then. Are those your tights?' Susan scooped up the unworn hosiery.

'Yes, I always bring a spare pair, in case I put my foot through the ones I'm wearing.'

'I like that colour. Where d'you get 'em?'

'Tesco's, I think.'

'Tell you what, shall I have these? Then I can get you another pair next time I'm round there.'

'All right,' Eileen gave in.

'See you outside.'

'Yes.'

Susan teetered away, pock-marking the floor with her five-inch heels.

'Didn't you want them tights?' enquired Valerie, the team's vice-captain, as she checked the room for lost property.

'Yes,' said Eileen. 'I did, really.'

Alice and Matthew were playing blow-football. Their efforts were not greatly helped by the presence of Lizzie, intent upon eating the ball.

'No, Lizzie,' squawked Matthew, wresting it from her groping fingers.

Lizzie, thwarted, gnawed at a goal-post.

'Oh, Grammar, she's got the goal-stick,' he appealed.

'Well, perhaps we should put it on the table.'

'You're not allowed to.'

'Oh, I don't think Mummy would mind.'

'It's against the rules.'

'Are you sure, dear? I didn't see anything about playing below sea-level.'

'But. . .' Matthew drew a deep breath and forgot what he was about to expound.

'Can I have a biscuit, Grammar?'

'I haven't got any, darling.'

'We have. Shall I get them? You can have one as well. But not Lizzie, or her tooth will fall out.'

'Thank you, darling, but I think I'll wait till tea-time. Why don't you?'

'Is it tea-time yet?'

'Not quite.'

'When is it?'

'In about three hours.'

'I might be hungry before then.'

'Well, let's wait and see, shall we? Is it my turn?'

A wild croaking issued from Lizzie's throat, where the plastic football was all but lodged. Alice upended her sharply and chopped at her shoulder-blades. The ball spun across the room, leaving a maroon and savage Lizzie grappling to pursue it.

'Lizzie is very naughty,' smirked Matthew.

Alice, more than a little shaken by the episode, gathered up the remnants of the game and transferred them to the crest of the *Observers*.

'But we can't play it there,' howled Matthew. 'There isn't any room with all that newspapers.'

'Do you want to go to the park?'

'Can I bring my scooter?'

'Yes, why not?'

Why not? reflected Alice, as the mechanical ruin hacked at her ankles. 'Because it is the oldest, heaviest, most malicious piece of rustic weaponry south of Newcastle.

It seemed to her that the park was designed to cause the most misery to the most people for the most time feasible. It was reached via two main roads, the traffic lights of which alternated in a way which rendered crossing at any given moment potentially fatal. Green men fluttered and blinked just long enough to allow the tribes of grannies, bikes and pushchairs to reach the middle of the North Circular, before snapping red as the juggernauts thundered past, spraying the flustered islanders with fumes and chocolate wrappers.

Once within the gates, exquisite gardens, sheltered from the winds but forbidden to children, opened on to a stretch of tarmac, criss-crossed by dogs fresh from the duck pond and large boys on larger BMX bikes, who skidded and spun around the hapless pedestrians pressing towards the playground.

The area reserved for swings and slides backed on to an expanse of grass which ran the length of the park and housed the wherewithal for sixteen football pitches. Alice had counted them once as she stood in frozen misery while Matthew clambered to the top of the rocket, only to discover he was unable to reverse the process. Fortunately, a sympathetic father had recognised the symptoms and hoicked him down before serious panic set in.

The winds which swept the playground came straight from

Siberia, or so Alice maintained, and few among the shivering adults huddled in the broken shelter disagreed with her. But the children loved it, and, after all, the fresh air was so good for them.

'Darling, wouldn't you like to ride your scooter for a bit?'

'I might get tired.'

'Well, you did want to bring it, Matthew, and I'm getting a bit tired of wheeling it. I have to push Lizzie as well, you see.'

'You can leave Lizzie by the fish.'

'Lizzie might not like that.'

'She will.' Matthew's lids shuttered affirmatively.

'If you're not going to ride your scooter, I think I'll put it down on the grass.'

'It might get stolen.'

'I shouldn't think so.'

'Our car did. The bandits took it while Mummy was cleaning her teeth.'

'Well, we've cleaned ours so I think it will be quite safe. Now go and have a swing if that's what you want.'

'I might fall off.'

'This is Gerry, Eileen. Gerry – Eileen. He's here for a month, then he and Gordon, – that's Gordon over there in the corner, the dopey-looking one – are going to Yugoslavia.'

'To live?'

'No, dumbo. For a holiday.'

'I've been to Italy. Rimini, as a matter of fact. With my sister, Jeanette. That was before we was married, mind you.'

'Did you marry your sister, then?' asked Gerry.

Eileen blushed. 'I mean before we got married. Jeanette married Bob and I married my husband.'

'Glad to hear you didn't marry someone else's. What are you drinking, Eileen?'

'Gin and lime, please, with lots of ice.' She fished in her purse and handed him a pound.

'Put it away, as the actress said to the archdeacon. Sue?'

'I'll have another Pink Lady.'

'Tut tut.'

'Shut it,' said Susan.

'Is he always like that?' Eileen asked when Gerry was gone.

Susan was trying to light a Rothmans with a disposable lighter. 'Like what?'

'Oh,' said Eileen, perplexed. 'Funny?'

'Our Gerry reckons he's the greatest thing since sliced bread,' wheezed Susan.

'He's very good-looking.'

'D'yer reckon? I must tell him.'

'No, don't, Sue,' Eileen implored.

Susan noted the reaction. 'How's your Dave? Haven't seen him for ages.'

'He's okay. Doing a lot of coaching.'

'Oh yeah?'

'Yeah. They've got kiddies' classes at the pool now. He's helping Giacomo with them.'

'Does Dave like kids?'

'Course he does.'

'Not all fellas do, you know. You remember that bloke from the garage I was going out with?'

'The one with different coloured eyes?'

'No, not him. He was in insurance. I saw him the other day down the market. He was buying a tray. He didn't see me. No, Derek. He couldn't stand kids. Do you know he once said if he had his way they'd all be drowned at birth. Just like kittens.'

'Didn't he like cats, either?'

'Can't have done I suppose.'

Eileen's lower jaw was trembling. 'Oh, that's awful, Sue. How could you go with a bloke like that?'

Susan considered. 'He was all right about other things. He bought me a lovely jersey for me birthday. You know, the one with the sheep in a field. That one.'

'I like that one,' sighed Eileen. 'Fancy not liking kids, though. I can't understand that.'

'What can't you understand, my lovely?' Gerry deposited the drinks, scattering Susan's sausage-flavoured crisps.

'Oh, Gerry, you are a lout. Don't they teach you nothing in the army?'

'Certainly they do. I can shoot a packet of Golden Wonder off the table with me feet behind me back. Shouldn't be eating them, anyway. You'll get fat, then no one'll want you. You'll be on the shelf.'

'Me and you both.'

'That's right. Couple of bookends. Ever thought of becoming a book, Eileen?'

'I don't read much.'

'You should, you know. Learn a lot from books, you can.'

'Not the kind you read, you can't,' interpolated Susan maliciously.

'My husband's always reading.'

'Is he? He sounds a very interesting man. How did you come to know our Susan, then, Eileen? She hasn't got many pretty friends. In fact, I'd go so far as to say you're her only pretty friend, but you certainly make up for the rest of them.'

'Oh shut up, Gerry. You're embarrassing her.'

'No, I'm not. Am I, Eileen? You can't help being the prettiest girl – woman, I should say – in the room.'

' 'Ere, Gordon, are you going to sit there like a stuffed potato and hear me insulted by me own lousy brother?' Gordon stirred in the corner, where he had been slumped for the better part of the evening, following a twenty-four hour celebration of his homecoming, and opened his mouth. Nothing, however, was forthcoming, and he was allowed to sink back as Gerry told two more jokes and suggested they all adjourn to Annie's when the bar closed.

Eileen said she must go home, and rose amid a howl of protests. She declined Gerry's offer to accompany her to the bus stop, but when Sue asked her if she would be at the practice next Friday, she recanted and said she expected so. Her cycle must look to itself.

Their lunch was progressing well.

Raymond, under Helen's giggling guidance, had ordered and enjoyed a *salade lyonnaise*, and was embarking on his main course when disaster struck. The Head of Overseas Planning (Europe) had just taken a large mouthful of his pigeon *à la catalane*, when his face was seen to contort. At least, Helen saw it, and shrank back aghast, as her companion sucked in his breath and clamped his hand to his mouth.

'What is it?' she breathed.

Very slowly Raymond removed his hand, as though convinced that his jaw would come with it. Gingerly his forefinger and thumb crept between his lips and probed furtively about his gums.

Even more slowly, they emerged, bearing a small grey ball.

Helen gasped.

Raymond had bitten the bullet.

Worse was to come. A second inspection produced, nestling between his fingers, a jagged white cone of porcelain.

Raymond had broken a crown.

With an ill-stifled groan, he made for the nearest *salle de bain*, where closer examination convinced him that a visit to the *musée* might be beneficially swapped for one to the *dentiste*.

Despite this obvious setback, Raymond was sufficiently man-of-the-world to decide that, however the incident might blight his intended flirtation, the meal was basically superb, and that vanity alone should not prevent its continuance.

Thus it was that young Helen Craig, plucked from the typing pool to be improved by Denis Roebuck, found herself sitting opposite a member of senior management in Normandy, gazing into his small green eyes, and rather more often into his crippled mouth, and basking in her newborn rapture.

'You were so vulnerable, she would murmur, mistakenly, later.

Raymond would smile bashfully and stroke her hair. 'I had only you to help me. My God, if I'd had to face that butcher on my own, he'd've sent me back as a lampshade.' Helen didn't fully understand the connotation, but she always laughed because she knew it was funny.

PRIÈRE DE S'ASSEOIR, ordered the notice. DÉFENSE DE FUMER.

'*Vous avez un rendez–vous, monsieur?*'

'*Non.*' Raymond's gestures were gratifyingly Gallic. '*J'ai cassé mon* tooth.'

'*Dent,*' Helen prompted.

'What? Oh, yes. *Voilà.*' Raymond exposed his gums.

Madame, who was obviously inured to the smell of garlic, recoiled not at all. '*Je comprends, mais vous devez prendre rendez–vous. Monsieur Baclaut est un homme beaucoup occoupé. Il a trop de clients. Toujours il travaillé. . .*' Her hands wafted tellingly about the empty room.

'What the hell does that mean?' snapped Raymond. For a moment he had forgotten Helen wasn't Ginny. He grinned lopsidedly. 'I mean, do you understand a word she's saying?'

'I think she wants you to make an appointment.'

'Why? Isn't he here?'

'I don't know. Wait a minute.'

Helen smiled bewitchingly at Madame, who was scouring a ledger. '*Madame,*' she cajoled, '*Je vous en supplie. Ce monsieur s'est cassé une dent en mangeant du pigeon. . .*'

Madame nodded. '*Ah oui, les plombs. Je sais. Ça arrive toujours.*' Her eyes had not risen. Helen tried again.

'*Madame, ce monsieur a besoin d'un dentiste d'urgence. Sa compagnie paiera. Ne vous inquiétez pas.*'

Madame surveyed Helen with distaste. '*C'est peut-être vrai, mademoiselle, mais ce n'est pas une question d'argent,*' *mais de temps. Monsieur Baclaut a déjà trop de clients. Il est fatigué, vidé. Ce n'est plus un homme, plutôt une ombre.'*

Even Raymond could not fail to appreciate the grandeur of such an outburst. He turned to Helen with a look of appalled surprise. She read it as a cry for help. The adrenalin churned once more. '*Madame,*' she appealed, her voice low with conspiracy, '*comprenez la situation. Monsieur s'est cassé une dent. S'il vous plaît, excusez moi, je dois vous expliquer les circonstances de notre visite.*' Still lower: '*La femme de monsieur va avoir un bébé d'un moment à l'autre. Il veut absolument être avec elle pour l'aider pendant l'accouchement.*'

Madame emerged from her ledger, '*Odent?*' she croaked. '*Sous l'eau?*'

'*Oui,*' Helen agreed vigorously.

'*Odent,*' repeated Madame, '*magnifique. Quel homme. Quel courage.*' Her moist eyes focused benignly on Raymond's bland features as she rose and padded to the baize door.

'What was all that about?' Raymond whispered hoarsely.

'I said your wife was pregnant and you wanted to help with the birth.'

'God forbid!' spluttered Raymond before he could help himself. Helen gazed at him curiously. 'I mean, what a splendid idea.' Helen smiled, unsure to which he referred.

Madame returned, her smile like a laser. '*Ne vous en faites pas. Monsieur Baclaut soignera ce monsieur.*'

Monsieur Baclaut was a plump, cheerful young man who spoke rather good English and fixed Raymond up with a temporary crown for eighty francs.

Roebuck was not entirely pleased to find Helen out. The clerk glumly informed him that the young lady had left soon after lunch with 'yewer frond from ternty-two' and had not yet returned. 'Der town as many interesting sarts,' he added, mournfully, as if to confirm Roebuck's worst suspicions. His ego denied the likelihood of an intelligent young woman preferring the company of a middle-aged hamster to his own. A large Martini swirling in his manly fist, he retired to his shower for ten minutes, nine of which were spent attempting to adjust the enigmatic dial to something between eleven and two hundred degrees Centigrade. Invigorated, if not refreshed, by his exertions, he sandwiched a pale apricot shirt between gaberdeen strides and a mild sports jacket, and rang through to number forty-three.

If Helen seemed a trifle evasive, pleading weariness and work, Roebuck was undaunted.

Duly they met in the cocktail lounge at eight fifteen. Helen wore a blue linen skirt and an embroidered blouse. Roebuck decided it might pass for '*la mode paysanne*' and banished the suspicion that she had worn it to work on Tuesday.

"I thought we'd have dinner at Le Bon Truffle and then go on to Sachette's. If that's not up to scratch we can always try Henri's, although I'm not sure that I should take an innocent young lady to such a den of iniquity."

Helen failed to ignite. She nodded vaguely and said, 'Whatever you think. I don't want to be too late."

"Wait till you've had a couple of glasses of *vin*. You'll buck up no end. Sure you won't be too warm in that skirt?"

'I can hardly take it off.'

Roebuck guffawed.

'What would you like to drink?'

'Could I have some Perrier, please?'

'Perrier?' Roebuck wondered how he could have been so wrong. Helen had always seemed rather go-ahead among the bevy of typists flitting about the buildings at JCV.

Their first encounter had been one afternoon in the lift, when she had lolled against him in a distinctly provocative manner. True, one of the girls was leaving to get married, and a hen party of some sort had obviously been taking place, but the look Helen cast him as they disentangled themselves convinced him that she was more than a little interested. Now here she sat in a mail-order skirt, drinking mineral water and muttering about early nights.

Roebuck tried again. 'Quite a good day for me. I think we've finally fixed the sealant quota. Shouldn't be any more trouble on that score.'

'Oh, good,' murmured Helen, plainly not listening.

'Bit of a feather in my cap, actually. Thought we might celebrate. Let our hair down.'

'Oh, good,' said Helen again.

'So, if you want to change. . .?'

'I'm fine, thank you. Unless you think I should?'

Roebuck was confounded. 'Actually, Helen. . .' he began, but her gaze had swivelled to the swing doors, through which Raymond, in a check shirt and flannels, was manoeuvring for the exit with an elderly female in a scarlet sari.

'Oh, here's Raymond.'

Raymond spied Helen's frantic wave and returned it. He stopped to speak to the barman, who pointed back to the swing doors. Raymond grimaced, seemed about to follow the man's flailing arm movements, then changed his mind and joined the pair.

'Evening, Roebuck. Sorry I'm late. Bloody shower. Left over from the Occupation, I shouldn't be surprised. One minute like an ice bucket, next you're being boiled alive. I spoke to the man, but. . .' he grinned at Helen, 'you know my French.'

'Hullo, Ray. What are your plans for this evening?'

'I asked Raymond to join us. I hope you don't mind?' Helen looked a little pink, but her eyes were fully on Roebuck. Roebuck opened his mouth and closed it again. 'No, of course not. Good idea. Right, who's for the Bon Truffle, then?'

'Right,' said Raymond. 'If you could just hang on a minute. I must ring Ginny.'

He got up. Roebuck watched Helen's face struggling with rapturous torment. 'Pity Ginny couldn't have come,' he scraped. 'You'd like her.' Still, despite his better feelings, he couldn't help smiling at Biggles' victory.

The dinner *à trois* went off reasonably well, with Raymond

choosing the wine, Helen translating the menu and Roebuck cracking the jokes. Tales of the boardroom were kept to a minimum because, after all, Helen was a junior, but the story of Raymond's tooth was tossed back and forth between the two protagonists till Roebuck began to feel like a spectator at Wimbledon.

'. . . And then you told her I wanted to deliver the baby myself. . .'

'Well, not exactly, but I did hint that. . .'

'Honestly, Roebuck, you wouldn't credit these dentists – empty waiting room, not so much as a toothbrush in sight. . .'

'He certainly didn't seem awfully busy. . .'

'Mind you, eighty francs is a bit steep, wouldn't you say?'

'He did fit you in, though. It was an exception. . .'

'And you are an exceptional young woman.' Raymond gazed rakishly at Helen, who blushed to the roots of her hair. Roebuck ordered more cognac, but the look had told him his presence was superfluous to their enjoyment, so he made his excuses and slipped away to Sachette's, to awake the following morning entwined with an ample chanteuse who giggled ferociously but couldn't tell him where his watch had gone.

Raymond and Helen sipped their liqueurs and studied the flower arrangement on their table. Without Roebuck a certain not unpleasant tension had sprung up between them, best eased by silence.

Raymond lit a cigar. 'Do you mind?'

'I love them – not to smoke, I mean. Just the smell.'

Raymond settled back. 'I'm really enjoying this trip,' he volunteered. 'How about you? Glad you came along?'

'Oh, yes,' sighed Helen. 'It's all I could've hoped for.' She glanced sideways and caught his appraising eyes. A little shiver of excitement ran through her as she thought about what the girls in the pool would say. But of course she would never tell them.

'We must have lunch,' mooted Raymond, as they crossed the Hoverport lounge. Helen smiled happily and murmured her assent.

'You're sure I can't offer you a lift?'

For a moment Helen seemed to waver, and Raymond's heart plummeted, but she shook her head resolutely. 'I must go to Auntie Jen's. She'd never forgive me if I didn't pop over while I'm down here.'

'Pity,' said Raymond, his glance implying rather more.

'Shall I see you on Monday?' Helen kicked herself for asking.

'I should say. That is, if I'm not at the dentist.' Raymond smiled and kissed her lightly on the cheek. She smelled lovely. On impulse he kissed her again, on the mouth. 'Bye, Helen.'

'Bye' – Helen's voice was husky with emotion – '. . . darling.'

Gerry picked Eileen up after the match, and Sue followed crossly in Gordon's Fiat.

'Did you win?'

'We drew. Two all.'

'Did you score any?'

'I can't, can I? I'm defence.'

'My defences are down,' crooned Gerry. 'And you've got me where you want me.'

'Where are we going?'

'Fancy a drink?'

'Don't mind.'

'Good. I know a lovely little pub by the river.'

'I don't know, Gerry. I don't want to be too late.'

'We won't be. Just one drink, then I'll take you home. I'd like to meet this husband of yours, anyway. The way Sue goes on about him, he sounds like an Olympic gold medallist.'

'Oh, he's nothing like that.'

Gerry caught the frisson and worked on it. 'Sue says he's fantastic. At sports and that. Swimming. Isn't he a professional or summat?'

'Sort of. He's a coach. At the pools. Talent spotter, I suppose you might call him.'

'Good bread?'

Eileen shot him a glance. 'Not bad. Why?'

'No reason. Just wondered why he'd take a dead-end job like that if it's not for the filthy lucre.' There was a pause. Eileen considered her nails.

'That's what I say,' she murmured.

Gerry relaxed.

Helen was very pretty, Raymond decided, watching her cross the restaurant to where he was waiting in the cluttered little alcove. She moved well. Smoothly, sinuously. Ginny always managed to catch her sleeve on the door knob, or her heel in the grating. She wasn't precisely clumsy, but she always seemed to be engaged in a running battle with the mechanics of existence. Other people managed to shut the doors of washing machines; with Ginny there was a six-to-four chance of it springing open during the final rinse. Her bedmaking was reminiscent of a fight with a hairy pancake, the blankets conspiring to be both chilly and suffocating.

He remembered Matthew's third birthday. The cake was supposed to be a hedgehog. Indeed it was. An excellent hedgehog. Ginny had trimmed and sculpted it into a remarkable chocolate facsimile. What if it were the size of a cupcake when she had finally relinquished the palette knife?

Helen sat down. 'Am I late?'

'No, I don't think so. Hardly.' He smiled.

Helen blushed. 'I was just finishing the circular. I wanted to get it done in case . . . I mean, I didn't want to have to go back to it this afternoon.'

The blush deepened.

Raymond imbibed it, then said soothingly, 'No, of course not. Anyway, you're not late. Campari?'

'Please.'

Raymond ordered aperitifs.

The waiter brought menus.

Helen tried to concentrate.

Raymond engrossed himself with the wine list.

The waiter returned.

'Have you decided?'

'Well, I think I'd like the *sole Véronique*.'

'Good idea. I'll have the *tournedos Rossini*.'

'And to start?'

'Avocado mousse, please.'

'Paté for me.'

The wine waiter loomed.

Raymond frowned. 'Of course you'd like white?'

'I don't mind. I like red . . . if you prefer.'

'Nonsense, child, you can't drink Burgundy with fish.' Raymond's eyes rolled heavenwards in what he hoped was mock horror.

Helen interpreted the shock as genuine.

'I don't mind. Honestly. You choose.'

Raymond chose.

Eileen thought she would die laughing. Tears, swimming in mascara, drenched her face, and a strange whinnying sound fought its way to the surface every time she managed to take a breath.

Susan was giggling too, but, as Eileen later reflected, she seemed to find the spectacle of Eileen's hysterics more amusing than the cause of them.

The cause of them was Gerry.

The two women had been endeavouring for some time to clarify the finer points of netball for him, but Gerry seemed incapable of grasping even the simplest rules.

'You see, the goal attack marks the goal defence.'

'Yeah?'

'And the wing attack marks the wing defence.'

'And what does the goal defence do?'

'Defends.'

'Defends what?'

'The goal.'

'Which goal?'

'Their goal.'

'Whose goal?'

'The goal defence's goal.'

'I thought the goal defence couldn't shoot.'

'She can't.'

'Well, how does she get a goal, then?'

'Not that goal, the other goal.'

'Oh, I see. The goal defence defends the goal she hasn't got, in case she had got one.'

'The goal attack gets the goal.'

'When she's not attacking the defence?'

'She doesn't attack the defence, she attacks the goal.'

'Even when she hasn't got one?'

'She's the one that gets them.'

'She shoots the goals?'

'She does if the shooter doesn't.'

'What does the shooter do?'

'She shoots.'

'She should join the army.'

Eileen's nose was hurting. She had never overcome a tendency to snort when more than mildly amused, and this attempt to bring Gerry up to date with modern netball was proving too much for her nasal membranes.

She made a last desperate effort to haul herself back to the fringes of sobriety.

'The point is, if Susan's the centre and I'm the goal attack. . .'

'Which you're not.'

'No, but if I was. . .' Eileen began to snuffle.

Susan broke in, 'I could pass to her, even if she was in the goal.'

'If she was in the goal you'd need the fire brigade to get her out.'

'Oh, Gerry, you swine,' shrieked Susan. 'You know what I mean. In the goal circle, that's what I mean.'

'Circle of gold,' mused Gerry. 'Talking of which, have either of you two ladies come across the circle of herpes? Now, I might consider joining that.'

Susan shrieked again, while Eileen, who did not know what herpes was, was able to draw breath and mop her still pretty, but extremely roseate face.

'Isn't he awful?' howled Susan. 'Circle of herpes. You can count us out of that one, can't he, Eileen?'

'Yes,' sniffed Eileen weakly. 'What is it?'

Susan's braying cackles scratched the fumey air like a lathe.

' "What is it?" ' she honked. 'She's not serious. Tell me she's not serious. someone. Gordon, tell me she's not serious. "What is it?" Did you hear that?' and Susan collapsed stiffly over her comatose beau.

Gerry leant towards the crimson Eileen, who sat battered

beneath this onslaught. He put his mouth rather close to her ear and said softly, 'Take no notice of her, love, she's had too much gin. No style, our Susan, even if she is my sister. Do you want another, or shall we go outside for a bit? It's like the Black Hole of Calcutta in here.'

Eileen stuttered that she ought to go home, but moving to pick up her coat she felt Gerry's hand on her arm. He said nothing but got up as she did, and without another look at the now peevish Susan, guided her across the room.

'Where d'you think you're going?' pealed after them and, as they passed out into the cool night air, Eileen just caught Susan's parting shot. 'She's a married woman, you know, is Eileen.'

Gerry led the way to the borrowed XR3 and unlocked the passenger door. He stood aside as Eileen got in.

'I can get a bus,' murmured Eileen. 'They stop outside Dickins and Jones. It's no trouble.'

Gerry's velvet eyes perused her thoughtfully for a moment, then he twitched the car into life.

'Don't do that,' he said. 'There's no need for that.'

'There you are.'

Helen looked up from the battle-worn filing cabinet, which was grimly denying her the records of a now defunct plastics factory.

'Oh, hallo,' she murmured.

Lindsey, a temp of four years' standing, gazed steadfastly into her ledger, as her ears swivelled aerial-like towards the pair.

'Were you looking for me?'

'As a matter of fact, yes,' Raymond boomed in an effort to sound casual. 'I was wondering if you knew anything about the Deptford scheme?' he bellowed. 'There's a chap coming over from Brussels on Tuesday, and it might be useful if you could come along to the meeting. Steer us through the language barrier, that sort of thing.'

Helen's blush deepened.

She really is a smasher, Raymond thought, watching her neck glow beneath the Chinese silk blouse.

'I really don't know a lot about it, apart from what Mr Roebuck mentioned on the ferry going over, but of course I'd be very happy to come to the meeting, if you think I'd be of any use.'

'Fine. Tell you what – ' but even Raymond could no longer be oblivious to Lindsey's tilted torso. She was straining so hard to hear, her body seemed in danger of keeling over.

'Never mind,' he shouted. 'Eleven o'clock, Tuesday. In my office. Come ten minutes early and I can fill you in.'

The choking splutters erupting from both Lindsey and her crony, Janine, caused Raymond to reflect momentarily on the subtlety of this remark. He smiled briefly and marched from the typing pool, leaving Helen to ponder the dubious delights of being in love with a clown.

Eileen was shaking.

She watched the car's rearlights sweep away into the distance, and still she stood where Gerry had deposited her: outside the block of flats where she and Mitchell lived.

She couldn't go in. What could she say to him? He'd be bound to notice. Unconciously she smoothed her skirt and fluffed up her bushy perm. Perhaps he'd be asleep. It was so late.

Supposing he wasn't? Surely he'd want to know where she'd been? Then she remembered her cover. 'At Susan's. We might go out for a drink. Why don't you come?'

'No thanks, love. I want to finish my book. Due back tomorrow. I've renewed it twice already.'

'Just as you like.'

Serve him right. He asked for it. How could he be so trusting? What did he take her for? She was only twenty-four. And she was pretty. Everyone said so. Except him. That wasn't fair. He did say so. But not very often. Not as often as Gerry.

Eileen went into the block.

The lift was broken.

Bitterly she stalked up the clanging stairway to the third floor. She was right. He had gone to bed. Couldn't even wait up for her. The relieved Eileen clattered angrily round the kitchen as she made her drinking chocolate.

It serves him right, she thought again as she indignantly sliced the coffee sponge. 'It serves him right.'

'What does?'

Eileen spun round to see Mitchell lolling drowsily in the doorway. His pyjamas fastened on the wrong buttons.

'What does what?'

'What serves him right?'

Eileen felt panic zipping through her. 'I don't know. What are you doing, creeping around like that in the middle of the night?'

'I wasn't creeping. You were playing the 1812 on your Horlicks mug. You didn't hear me. Can I have a piece of that?'

Eileen became awkwardly aware that she had cut twelve slices of cake. 'Now look what you've made me do,' she jittered. 'It'll go stale now.'

'I'll have two pieces, then. Come on, love, come to bed. You look worn out. It's all right' – as Eileen slithered away from him – 'I've no evil intentions.'

Eileen slid past him with what she hoped was credible sangfroid. 'I prefer the morning, anyway.'

As she lay in the steaming bath, Eileen closed her eyes and thought about Gerry and the back of the borrowed Escort.

'Oh, Christ,' she murmured. 'What have I done?'

This time Mitchell didn't hear, but before he fell asleep he reflected on his wife's bright, nervy eyes and staccato cake-carving.

'I wonder if she's ill,' he thought, 'or something.'

'I thought that went very well,' Raymond commented as he returned to his desk. 'You were a great help.'

Helen smiled happily.

Why mention that Monsieur Lafaut spoke immaculate English? After all, she had reminded them that the new contracts were likely to be subject to changes in the Health and Safety Laws if they were not completed before 31 March.

They had been most grateful. Particularly Raymond, who had tapped the side of his head in a friendly, almost fatherly manner when she finished speaking.

'Of course,' he had said. 'Quite right. Thank you, Miss Craig.' That was when he had tapped his head.

'I think I owe you a lunch.'

'Oh, no,' said Helen. 'Really, you don't. Not another one.'

Raymond looked a little shocked at this rebuff and Helen was afraid for a moment that her lowliness had betrayed her.

'What I mean is, I'd love to, but I can't keep letting you buy me lunch – it's not fair. I ought to buy you lunch.'

'All right,' said Raymond. 'You buy me lunch. And I'll buy you dinner.'

They both laughed.

Ginny put down the phone.

'That was Raymond. He won't be home till late.'

'Work?'

'I suppose so.'

Alice discarded the wool she was trying unsuccessfully to wind. She was not greatly helped by Matthew, who had insisted on holding the yarn for her but was unwilling to abandon his game of skittles while doing so.

Lizzie immediately pounced upon the ball and dipped it in her yoghurt.

'Oh, Lizzie, you are horrid. How can I make you a pretty hat if you make the wool all sticky?'

Ginny, having seen the pattern, thought Lizzie probably knew what she was doing, but she clucked reprovingly out of fondness for Alice.

'Does he still play squash?'

'Now and again.'

'You should both go. You always used to.'

'There are a lot of things we always used to.'

Alice was rinsing her wool in the sink.

'Shall I make some more tea?'

'I'll do it. You sit down. You haven't had a moment's rest since you arrived.'

'I don't come here to rest.'

'Just as well. Do you want a piece of toast? I'm going to have one.'

'All right. No, actually, I don't think I will, dear.' This as Ginny took her home-made brick from the bread bin and began to saw.

'When are you going to Eric and Rosie's?'

Alice winced. 'Next Thursday. Rosie's picking me up after lunch.'

'I thought her car was bust.'

'She's got another. A Sierra, I think she said it was called. Is there such a thing?'

'I think so. The last one I hit had that sort of name.'

'Not Rosie's?'

'No, unfortunately. Are you sure you don't want some toast?'

'Quite sure, thanks.'

'What about a drink?'

'I thought you were making tea.'

'Which would you like?'

'Well, only a very small one.'

'How about a liqueur?'

'Do you think I could have a Cointreau?'

'I'm sure you could.'

Raymond gestured to the waiter. 'Cointreau, and an Armagnac for me, please.'

They sat in silence, watching the glowing logs in the Jacobean fireplace.

'This is the most beautiful place,' Helen began. 'How did you find it?'

Raymond coughed. 'I've er – been here once or twice,' he said. 'Used to belong to the Grevilles, but they sold it to some American who sold it to one of the Rothschilds and finally the National Trust took it over, but they agreed to lease part of it out as a restaurant to Jarvis Copeland.'

'I think it's lovely.'

'I think you're lovelier.' Raymond took her hand and kissed her fingers gently.

Helen forgot it was only an infatuation.

'I must take you home.'

They had finished their drinks and Raymond had paid by Diners Club. They spoke little, driving through the Surrey countryside. The night was very starry and Helen leant back against the headrest and gazed up at the sky.

She knew they weren't in London when the car slithered smoothly to a halt. The next she knew was Raymond's bristly mouth bearing down upon hers, and his expensive tweed arms engulfing her.

When he delivered her eventually to her flat in Wood Green his eyes were ablaze with ungratified passion. Helen leant dreamily on his shoulder.

'Do you want to come in for a coffee?'

Raymond straightened up. 'I won't, thank you, Helen, if you don't mind. Much as I'd like to.'

'I understand.' Helen cooed, and kissed him softly on the mouth. Raymond purred and seemed about to pounce again, but Helen was chilly and had started to look for her latchkey. He waited till she had disappeared up the stairs, and then drove home.

When is Ginny going to realise? Emma wondered, as she watched her friend cheerfully unsetting Raymond's place at the table.

'I'm glad about that,' said Ginny. 'Now we can bitch about Sally and James. Raymond always likes to pretend gossip offends him, though from what I've heard about his office he could sponsor a column in the *Sun*. D'you know, the personnel manager had a vasectomy the morning after his secretary got the result of her pregnancy test? He must think they can be backdated.'

Emma laughed. 'What's Ray up to this time?'

'Work, he says. He does seem to be doing a lot of overtime at the moment. Still, it's their busy season. It's always like this between now and May.'

'It must be boring for you.'

'I have my books and my music.'

Emma laughed more genuinely. 'And your newspapers.'

'And them.'

'Do you ever read any of them, or is it just insurance against amnesia?'

'More like insurance against being thrown on the streets. Did you know newsprint is extremely warm, if worn close to the major arteries?'

'I must remember that.'

'And it does stop the scouts trying to clean my car.'

'How so?'

'They can get two pounds fifty a ream for these at Bentley's. Much more lucrative.'

Ginny placed the lasagne on the table.

'This looks nice.'

'Red or white?'

'Whichever.'

'Both.'

Raymond came in at eleven, and was not surprised, or even disgruntled, to see Emma and Ginny, arms tight round each other's necks, practising the art of self-defence, as depicted in an elderly *TV Times*.

'Hullo, Ray,' gurgled Emma. 'Lovely to see you. You're looking well. Aaagh. . .'

Ginny had taken advantage of this greeting to twist her leg round Emma's unwary thigh, and was now in the process of forcing her on to the parquet.

'What on earth are you two doing?'

'We're defending ourselves. What does it look like?' yelped Ginny, who was already regretting having taken an offensive which seemed to indicate the inevitable sacrifice of her right leg. 'Emma doesn't want to be mugged on the way home.'

'Hasn't she got the car?' asked Raymond solicitously. 'I'll run you home, Emma. No need to go on a stretcher.'

'Of course she's got the car,' whimpered his wife. 'Don't you know that more rapes and muggings take place on your own doorstep than anywhere else?'

'Is that why you leave the papers out?' asked Raymond uncharitably. 'Soft landing?'

'That's about it,' said Ginny miserably.

The room iced over.

'I'll get my coat,' said Emma.

'Watch you play squash?'

'Yes', said Raymond. 'That is, if you'd like to. We could get a bite to eat afterwards, then I'll run you home.'

'Thank you,' Helen replied uncertainly. 'That would be lovely.'

I don't want to do this, she thought as she dawdled moodily to the powder room at a quarter past five. I don't like squash and he won't win and what shall I say then?

'Hi, Helen,' called Lindsey, 'Are you coming to Chris's wine and cheese thing tonight?'

Helen gaped. 'I'd forgotten about that,' she admitted. '*And* I promised to help with the food.'

'So what's stopping you?'

'Nothing. That is, I'm supposed to be doing something else. Overtime.'

Lindsey was on the scent. 'Who for?'

'Slimey Samson.'

'I thought he was away.'

'He is. He asked me before he went. . .'

'Well, he's not due back till Friday. Do it tomorrow.'

'I can't. I'm having my hair cut.'

'Again?'

'Look, Lindsey, say sorry to Chris for me, would you? I'll make it up to him some other time.'

'He'll be ever so upset.'

'No, he won't,' Helen snapped. 'It's only lumps of cheese, for heaven's sake.'

Roebuck guffawed. 'What d'you mean, he beat you?'

'As God is my witness' Des reported ruefully. 'Mind you, I'd had a couple of lagers first, but I always do when I'm playing Ray. Can't stand a massacre.'

'Sure it was only a couple?'

'I tell you, the man played like a demon. He must have lost a stone in the first set. I was half afraid he'd have a coronary.'

The image of Raymond Jeavons playing squash like a demon was too much for Roebuck, who choked on his beer. When he had recovered sufficiently to draw breath he wiped his eyes and croaked, 'I don't suppose there was anyone watching, was there?'

'Not so far as I know. I was running too much to see. Why? Do you think he'd brought a talent scout?'

Roebuck grinned knowingly. 'Something like that,' he chortled.

'You were marvellous.' Helen took the proffered arm demurely. 'I never realised. . .'

'I could play?'

'. . . What an exciting game squash is. I've never really watched it before. It's so fast. How you ever manage to hit the ball is beyond me.'

Raymond had heard this remark before, but usually with a somewhat different emphasis. Now he received it with dignity.

'It's just a matter of being fit. Fancy a drink? There's a nice little pub in Charles' Court. They do food, too. Sound all right?'

'Sounds lovely,' sighed Helen.

This time Raymond did come upstairs.

The flat was surprisingly attractive, with old pine furniture and a proper-sized bath. The walls were papered in small, rather whimsical patterns – mainly flowers – and perhaps it all seemed a little twee and dainty for his taste, but Helen produced Glenfiddich and a decent crystal goblet, causing Raymond to decide that it was only 'the feminine touch' of the place which unsettled him.

'This is very nice.'

'The whisky?'

'The whisky, certainly, but I meant your flat. It's much. . .'

'. . . nicer than you expected?'

Raymond laughed cautiously. 'I didn't know what to expect.'

'And now you do?'

Helen seemed much more confident on her own territory, assertive even. He watched as she poured herself a Campari and soda.

'Why do you drink that stuff?'

'Have you ever tried it?'

'I don't think I have.'

'It's wonderful.' She slid to the ground by his feet and wafted the glass towards him. 'Taste.' Raymond gulped at the vermilion fluid.

'Well?'

'Wonderful.' His arms hauled her purposefully towards him, Helen neatly contriving to park the Campari before their tongues entwined. Then, a latter day Ariadne, she manoeuvred him through the Pierrot scatter cushions to her Laura Ashley bedroom.

Ginny was making bread when Raymond got in.

Ponderously she thumped the mass of glutinous dough which crouched beneath her fists like a battle-weary sloth.

'Aren't you meant to let it rise first?'

'I have let it rise. I'm shaping it, ready for the oven.'

'Shall I turn it on for you?'

Ginny looked up in bland surprise. Raymond's face was rather red and his small eyes were shining. He's been drinking, she thought.

'If you like. Two hundred and twenty.'

Raymond poured himself a glass of Perrier water.

'By the way,' he let drop, 'I beat Des.'

'Did you? What was the score?'

'Three-love.'

'Well done.'

'You don't sound very pleased.'

'More like surprised, I suppose.'

Raymond set down his glass. He glared at Ginny angrily.

'Why surprised? I've beaten him before.'

'When?'

'You know very well I've beaten him before. Often.'

'If you say so.'

'Are you calling me a liar?'

Ginny stopped torturing her bread. 'Do you want me to?'

'I'm asking you a question. Answer it, please.'

'All right, you're a liar. You have never, to my knowledge, beaten Desmond Raikes at squash, at tennis, at promotion or at buttoning your flies, which, incidentally, appear to be open.'

Why Raymond hit her, he was never completely sure. He had never done it before and it wasn't very hard. In fact, in keeping with most of his physical activities, it was uncoordinated and almost missed.

Ginny put her hand to her cheek and pressed it as though applying a tourniquet.

Raymond stood aghast for several seconds, then stepped falteringly towards her. 'Ginny. . .' he began.

Ginny waved him away. 'Leave me alone. Go away.'

'I didn't mean to. It was an accident. You just annoyed me.'

A single tear dripped on to the defeated loaf which Ginny was transferring to a tin.

'I can be annoying,' she said, and adjusted the regulo, which Raymond had set too high.

'What's the matter?'

Helen seemed a bit edgy, not her usual melting self. Almost as though she didn't want him to touch her.

'Nothing.' She dodged away again, nervously snatching up a mug with a weeping harlequin for a handle.

It was Saturday afternoon and Raymond had spent a tedious morning in Hammersmith helping Ginny buy shoes for the children.

Why she should have chosen a Saturday to go in search of the least amenable item of a child's accoutrement was beyond him. Also beyond him was her insistence that he accompany the surly party, unless it bore some reference to his passing remark that he was sure he could get size four shoes for less than ten pounds ninety-nine.

They had set off earlyish to avoid the crowds, if not the rain, and predictably had run into the largest horde of belligerent bargain-hunters since the collapse of Brentford Nylons.

Lizzie had been trodden on while trying to mould a Wellington round a basket-on-wheels, and Matthew had been proved to have one foot a size and a half wider than the other, necessitating the purchase of some singularly sinister trainers encrusted with the legend 'Brits are Best'. As the Head of Overseas Planning (Europe), Raymond felt bound to protest at such blatant jingoism, but the assistant, who was from Bangladesh, seemed unable to follow his drift, and replied balefully that they were the only one's in Matthew's size.

At a quarter past twelve Raymond pronounced himself satisfied with the morning's work, having spent a mere twenty-four pounds forty, and suggested that he might now be allowed to 'get over to Des's', where he planned to watch the rugby. Ginny conceded, and was left to cart the starving offspring back to Acton on the tube, which was now swarming with Chelsea supporters going the wrong way.

'You watch your rugby match,' said Helen. 'I'll make some coffee. Or would you rather have a drink?'

Raymond pottered doggedly after her. 'I'd rather have you.' His hands fumbled with her hair, but again she retreated, half-smiling, half-irritated.

'Go on. Sit down. You'll miss the beginning.'

'Not if we're quick.'

What an appalling thing to say, he realised. Helen looked palpably shocked. He sought a solution. 'I'm only joking, darling. What's rugby compared to an afternoon in bed with you? Besides, I can always see it on BBC2 tomorrow.'

The doorbell rang. Helen leapt away from him.

'Who's that?'

'I've no idea. Probably the bailiff.'

'Aren't you going to see?'

'Yes. Of course I am.' Helen braced herself and crept apprehensively into the hall. Raymond was mildly perplexed and not a little frustrated, but his born-again optimism was not readily crushed, so he shrugged manfully and turned on the television.

'Oh, hello.' A man's voice; then Helen again.

'Do you want to come in for a moment?' Obviously he did, for the door closed and the sound of their footsteps approached.

Raymond tried to look casual as he turned to greet the intruder. Helen stood behind the man, pink and miserable.

He wore an ill-fitting gravy-coloured suit with wide lapels, and a blue nylon shirt from which dangled a checked tie, encompassing as many colours as could usefully be said not to go together. A huge Rolex handcuffed his wrist, and his beringed fingers served only to emphasise the grit beneath his nails.

'Who's this, then?' asked the man, winking at Raymond.

'This is Raymond.' said Helen with an air of finality.

'Pleased to meet you, Raymond,' said the man. 'Come on, Helly, introduce us. Or are you shy all of a sudden?'

Helen looked as though she were going to be sick.

'I'm her father,' confided the stranger. 'But don't you worry. I won't say a word to her mum.' He tapped the side of his nose.

'I don't know what. . .' Raymond began, but Helen sliced across them both.

'Jack is my stepfather. He married Mummy when I was fifteen.' Mortification dripped from every syllable.

'The boxes are in the kitchen, Jack. Please take them now. We want to watch the rugby.'

Jack looked only mildly disconcerted by this. 'Oh, come on, Helly. Give us a cuppa something. I've come straight from work. Your boyfriend won't mind, will you, Ray?'

Raymond was torn between a wish to be rid of the interloper and a powerful curiosity to know more about his rôle in Helen's life.

'All right. Sit down. It'll have to be coffee. I've run out of tea bags.' Helen obviously wasn't going to waste her Lapsangh on Jack.

'Coffee'll be great, love. My throat's as dry as a you-know-what.' Again he winked. Since it was the same eye, Raymond decided it was probably a nervous tic, and cleared his throat noisily.

'Known Helly long, have you?'

'Quite a while. We work for the same company.'

'Aah. The famous JCV. Where all the men wear suits and play badminton.'

'Not at the same time, I hope.' Raymond laughed jerkily.

'Married, are you?'

Seeing Raymond baulk, Helen swept back into the room and practically hurled the mug at her stepfather.

'You'd better hurry. Mummy's probably waiting to go out.'

'That's all right. I can always give her a tinkle, can't I? So long as I leave the ten p.'

The wink.

'I daresay you've noticed, our Helen is very sharp about getting her dues. I'll be lucky if I get this for less than a quid. And there's no cream.'

'If you don't like it, don't drink it.'

'Do I get anything back on the empty?'

Helen turned to Raymond. 'Jack is referring to the time he knocked my Minton teapot off the dresser and I asked him to pay for another.'

'It's true, you know.' Jack's hand gripped Raymond's arm conspiratorially. 'And the joke of it is, I gave it her in the first place. Bloody Christmas present.'

'You didn't. You never gave me anything. It was Mummy.'

'Well, where d'you think *she* got the money from? Publishing her bloody poems?'

'Don't sneer at things you know nothing about. Mummy's poems are very good. Some of them.'

'They don't even rhyme.'

There was a silence. Raymond cleared his throat again.

'I paid for all this, you know,' Jack boasted. 'Got a few paper shops. I expect you noticed, there's one down below. I've got a Paki couple in there at the moment. Good workers, these Asians, you know. Not clock-watchers. Well, I don't suppose many of them can tell the time.'

This amused Jack inordinately. So much so that he spilt his coffee.

Helen mopped it up, her lips tight with disgust.

Raymond had never seen her face so strained. She looked quite old. He felt a great wave of tenderness for her. He wanted to cuddle her and tell her it didn't matter; that the appalling Jack only increased his feeling for her. She was so completely vulnerable as she fought for her self-respect.

He stood up sharply. 'What about these boxes, then? I'll give you a hand to get them down the stairs. Have you got a car?'

Jack looked confounded. 'No rush, Ray. As I said. . .'

'Actually, there is a bit. Helen and I have some things to talk about. I think you take my meaning.'

Jack's brow furrowed. 'It seems to me, mate, that you are asking me to get out of me own daughter's flat.'

'That's about the size of it.'

'Now, look here. . .'

'Yes?'

Slowly Jack's face spread into a slimy grin. 'Okay, mate. A nod's as good as a wink. In the kitchen, are they, Helly?'

Helen nodded.

As Raymond slammed down the Daimler's boot on the last carton, Jack, who had started the engine, wound down the window and said, 'Thanks, mate. Have a nice day. By the way, what's she like? I've always fancied our Helly. Reckon she must be quite a raver when she's going.' Then, face smarmy with imagined conquests, he drove away.

Helen was watching the rugby when Raymond returned. He knew she didn't understand it from the way her eyes fidgeted about the screen, trying to fix on some common denominator which would suddenly make sense of the mud-drenched turmoil.

He sat down beside her and put his arm round her waist. She sat very stiffly, eyes glued to the set.

'Are you enjoying this?'

'Oh, yes. It's very interesting.'

'Who's winning?'

Helen was flummoxed. 'I'm not exactly sure.' Her clear grey eyes looked up at him, like a child caught out in a lie. Then the warm tears came seeping out, quietly filing down her cheeks to wait their turn before dripping lemming-like off her chin to land on her Benetton jersey. Raymond watched solicitously for a few moments, then took out his man-sized tissue and mopped gently.

Helen hiccuped sorrowfully and buried her damp face in his sports jacket.

'He's so horrible,' she squeaked miserably.

'He is rather.' Raymond concurred. 'But it doesn't matter. There's no need to get upset about him. He's not worth it.'

'No, he's not.' Helen sneezed violently. 'But you see, Mummy thinks he is. At least, I think she does. . .' This last thought preoccupied her sufficiently to allow her tears some respite. 'She can't love him. It's not possible. He's so. . .'

'Horrible.' Raymond finished, and they both smiled.

'I'm so ashamed.'

'Why? He's nothing to do with you. Not even a relation.'

'A stepfather's a relation.'

'Only by marriage, not by blood.'

'It's the same thing.'

'No,' he drew her closer, 'it isn't. He isn't even related to your mother. So you see,' he kissed her forehead softly, 'you have nothing to be ashamed of.'

'I love you,' said Helen.

'You hardly know me.'

'I do. I've known you all my life. You're all I've ever wanted in a man.'

Raymond's head told him to get up and leave now. His vanity, not to mention his loins, told him to stay.

'You can't be sure of that.'

'I can. I am. I'd do anything for you. I'd even kill.'

Raymond smiled protectively. 'No need for that. What you need,' he kissed her ears, 'is someone to look after *you*.'

Helen melted.

Later, as he made his way home, Raymond thought My God, what have I done?

'Why, Ray, honey,' trilled Ginny in her best Milwaukee accent, 'just look at these darling pipes. Fancy them having central heating all those years ago. Don't that beat all!' Raymond sank lower in his borrowed Barbour and wished their hosts had not insisted on this trip to Dover Castle.

It was all right for them. Vicky and George's children were a good deal older and proportionately more civilised than theirs. It really was a bit much to expect a boy of four and a baby to appreciate the finer points of Tudor architecture. Not to mention the Waterloo Room, where they had lingered for twenty minutes, heads bowed over the amorphous reconstruction. Its all-pervading chaos reminded Ginny of Matthew's room after a visit from his friend Darren.

Beaty and Patrick peered dutifully down at the murky soldiers while their mother recited croakily from the explanatory panels adorning one end of the hall.

'Goodness, darling, did you know that if Marshal Grouchy hadn't been late finishing his breakfast, the whole battle might have swung the other way. Trust the Italians. No sense of time.'

'Grouchy wasn't an Italian, Vicky, my love, he was a frog. Patrick, where are you now?'

'I'm just by the East Ridge, Daddy. The Scots Greys are hacking up d'Erlon's left flank.'

Ginny winced.

'What? That can't be right. That didn't happen till fifteen hundred hours. We're only up to twelve hundred fifty. Stupid boy. You should be over there with Beaty waiting for Jerome's second attack on the Hougoumant. I say, Ray, I don't think young Matty should be sitting up there, old chap.'

Raymond swivelled to find his son spreadeagled along the Allied Line plastering cough sweets across the glistening expanse. 'Honestly, Matthew, what are you up to? Get down at once.'

'I can't,' returned the prostrate child, 'I'm too high.'

'Well, how did you get up there? Ginny, get him off, will you? Before he goes through the glass.'

Ginny, engaged in transferring Lizzie from reins to buggy, gazed at her husband with ill-concealed loathing. Raymond recognised the row-potential in repeating his request, so, groaning slightly in case anyone had forgotten his strained ligament, he slid an arm under his sprawling offspring and scooped him off the battlefield.

'But, Daddy, now I can't see it. I can't see the fighting now.' Sticky fists scrabbled at the showcase as Matthew strove to reinstate himself.

'There's nothing to see. Only a few tin soldiers. You've got plenty of those at home.'

'No, I haven't. I have't got any.'

'Well, you've got Lego. It's the same thing.'

'No, it's not. Lego isn't soldiers. Why can't I see it? Patrick's allowed.'

'Patrick isn't climbing all over it.'

'He's got big legs.'

'What about a postcard? Come on. I'll treat you. You can choose. I say, George, I'm just going to take Matthew to buy a postcard. Meet you back at the car.' The two of them strode off. Ginny rose limply from her encounter with Lizzie and the safety harness and wondered for the fifteenth time how soon they could decently depart for Acton.

Vicky was still droning on, trailed by a respectful cluster of Japanese businessmen who evidently took her for the official guide.

Lizzie began to howl. George glanced reprovingly at Ginny, before continuing a rather petulant discussion with

Patrick concerning the deposition of the Brunswicks and the Guards.

'I think I'd better go and find those two,' Ginny mooted brightly.

'Righto,' George concurred with alacrity. 'We'll be in the gallery. If you miss us we'll all meet up at the car.'

'Right. Won't be long.' Ginny trotted off, firm in her intention of finding a cup of tea.

Instead she found Raymond and Matthew, guiltily devouring ice pops in the shadow of the keep.

'How did you escape?' Raymond asked, wiping raspberry syrup from his pullover.

'I said I was going to look for you two. Did you get a postcard?'

'No, Matthew said he'd rather have a lolly.'

'Well, you'd still better get one. They're bound to want to inspect it.'

A hideous cry rent the air. Lizzie had noticed Matthew's ice pop. 'All right, darling. We'll get you one. I want a cup of tea, anyway. I'm parched.'

'Couldn't you wait till we get back? Vicky's bound to make one.'

'That's what I'm afraid of. Another sip of that embalming fluid and I shall throw up.'

'It is a bit weak.'

'It tastes like talcum powder. Probably is – some of her surplus.'

'Well, we'd better get a move on. They won't stay inside forever.'

'They've gone to look at the gallery. I expect George will redesign the patio when he gets home.'

'Come on, then.'

They bought Lizzie an ice cream and were creeping stealthily towards the cafeteria when a loud cry of 'Hoooo there' froze them in their tracks. George and family came blinking into the sunlight, eyes shielded against the glare. 'Can't see a thing,' roared George breezily. They managed to spot us, Ginny ruminated glumly as they were frog-marched back to the car park.

'I don't know about you lot,' chirped Vicky as they drove away, 'but I could do with a nice cup of tea.'

Ginny watched Lizzie fall.

One minute she was goose-stepping round the kitchen brandishing a stick of rhubarb, the next she had crumpled, a round bundle of baby, capsized by the jutting quarry tiles.

At first Ginny thought she was all right, but when Lizzie's head cleared the floor, the cry was too long in coming. She scooped the child up and saw blood splashing from her forehead. For a second she watched, then hauling up her skirt she forced it against the wound as the next wail issued, strange and lonely.

Matthew's huge eyes focused on the spectacle.

'Raymond,' Ginny shouted through the kitchen door. 'Lizzie's hurt herself.'

Raymond descended the ladder from which he was ineffectually trying to mend the gutter.

They drove quickly, without speaking, Matthew stowed in the back like a captive rabbit, half-eaten Crunchie clenched in his dimunitive fist.

Lizzie was conscious but silent; the blood was no longer flowing freely and beneath the matted tufts a purple egg was taking shape.

At reception the woman asked where they had come from.

'Acton. She tripped over the quarry tiles in the kitchen.'

'You realise this isn't your catchment area?' Encouraged by their mortified silence, she added, 'By rights you should be at the Central Middlesex.'

Raymond turned rather pale. 'What do you tell the motorway pile-ups? Some of them may have come from Plymouth.'

'Is it a bad cut?'

'We were rather hoping someone here might tell us that.'

'May I have the child's full name.'

'Elizabeth Maria Jeavons.'

'Date of birth.'

'Ninth of August 1982.'

'Any history of epilepsy or fits?'

Raymond seemed about to set the precedent.

'Take her over there. I'll do this.' Ginny urged. He seemed not to hear, then briskly he swept Lizzie out of his wife's arms and strode across the room, trailing the bewildered Matthew, who was coated in dissolving Crunchie.

'Any history of diabetes, tuberculosis, diphtheria?'

'No.'

'Is she allergic to anything?'

Bureaucrats apart? thought Ginny. 'I don't know. I don't think so.'

'Follow the green line.'

'I beg your pardon?'

'Follow the green line along the floor.'

Ginny peered downwards. Three streaks of marking tape stretched away, apparently all leading to the same place. She gestured to Raymond and Matthew, who rose in unison.

'We have to follow the green line.'

'Follow the yellow brick road,' shrilled Matthew, to the amusement of two blacks, who sat with identical wounds corrugating their foreheads. Ginny's attention was distracted by the sight of a student nurse whom Raymond had waylaid en route for the wards. Swiftly the girl disappeared into a cubicle, returning with a large wad of lint and some plaster, which she deftly affixed to the baby's temple before speeding once more on her way.

With equal dexterity Lizzie now applied herself to its removal.

The green line ground to a halt beside a cubicle adorned with posters warning against the use of blunted needles and infected swabs.

They sat down.

Matthew reorganised a trolley and daubed chocolate on the 'No Smoking' sign.

A man in a white coat appeared.

'Are you a doctor?'

'No.'

He disappeared.

Two nurses came in, smiled at Matthew and retreated.

A coloured woman in mauve asked Ginny if she'd opened her bowels that day.

Ginny asked why and she replied that the doctor needed to know.

'In that case I would prefer the doctor to ask me.'

'He's a very busy man.'

'Not too busy, it would seem, to ask fatuous and impertinent questions.' Ginny's voice had risen several decibels.

A ginger-haired man appeared.

'Mrs Wetherall?'

'No.'

'I beg your pardon. You're not Mrs Wetherall?'

'No.'

'You're not in labour?'

'I'm not in labour, neither is my husband, neither is my four-year-old son. My daughter, however, is bleeding from the head, and I think you would do your profession a service if you concerned yourself a little more with the living and let the future generation look to itself.'

Raymond opened the front door and Ginny carried in the sleeping Matthew.

Lizzie, sporting two stitches and an iced bun, trotted cheerfully behind.

Raymond poured two large whiskies and handed one to Ginny as she settled Matthew amongst the papers on the couch.

'Thank God that's over.'

'If that's Casualty, no wonder you wait four years for a bed.'

'Yes, and that's only if you're in labour.'

Raymond laughed and crossed to the french windows.

'The grass needs cutting.'

'Nonsense. The house is too short.'

Raymond walked back to the whisky and Ginny saw his eyes filled with tears.

She thought: It's because of Lizzie. And, of course, it was.

'We've got a flat. Or rather, Helen has. Her father owns a newsagents. There's a place over the shop we can have for a while.'

'Where is it?'

'Wood Green.'

Ginny didn't look up. She was dicing vegetables for a stir-fry.

'When will you go?'

'It's up to you. I thought perhaps – the end of the month?'

'Calendar or lunar?'

'Saturday week. If that's all right with you.'

This time Ginny did look at him. Raymond thought, As if she's never seen me before.

'Ginny. . .'

'Yes?'

'I'll see you're all right. All of you. . .'

'Thank you.'

'I'm afraid I've rather sprung this on you.'

'It is a surprise, certainly.'

'Would you rather I ate out?'

'The Meyricks are coming.'

'Oh, yes. Of course. I'd better get changed.'

'Yes.'

'Daddy. Daddeee. . .'

'What is it, Matthew? I thought you were in bed.'

'I am, but Lizzie won't let me be asleep.'

'Why not?'

'She's singing a hum.'

'I'd better go up.'

'Yes.'

Ginny saw that she had cubed a piece of soap.

Helen scanned the Ploughman's Arms. She saw Janine and Lindsey curved over their Slimlines in the window seat and, fearing recognition, slipped through the saloon.

Raymond was standing by the bar, deep in conversation with a muscley young man.

Halfway across the room her courage failed her and, gazing wistfully at Raymond's receding hairline, she retreated to the canteen.

What did it matter, anyway? In ten days' time Raymond would be permanent. She would be the centre of his world. Not Ginny, not the children, not the office, even, nor the red-headed stranger.

Raymond stared hard at Mitchell.

'To tell the truth, I don't know how it happened.' he said. 'At least, I know how, but I don't know why.'

'You're saying you wish it hadn't?'

'No, I'm not. Nothing of the kind. It's just that it's all been rather sudden. I didn't really intend. . .'

'To get copped?'

'Helen – that's the girl – is a fantastic creature, don't misunderstand me. She's intelligent, attractive, sensitive, all the things. . .'

'Your wife isn't?'

'No. My wife is intelligent. She's very attractive . . . in a messy sort of way. No dress sense. You know, she once turned up at JCV in, well, I don't know what they were really – sort of Bermuda shorts with braces. We ended up in the Kardomah.'

'Helen knows how to dress?'

'Oh yes. She works for JCV.'

'So you're leaving your wife because you've found someone who dresses better.'

Raymond straightened up. 'I'm sorry. I've been boring you.'

'That's all right. My wife thinks I'm impotent.'

'Are you?'

'Not so's you'd notice.'

'I'm going to miss the children. We've got two. Matthew's four and Lizzie. She's fourteen months. She's a terror. Into everything. You know, the week before last, I don't know how, but she got into my briefcase. She ate a report on Solihull marketing techniques. Fourteen pages. Fortunately I had a copy. Helen had to retype it on Sunday evening. She was very good about it.'

'Children are like that, I suppose.'

'Yes. In a way it'll be a relief to be out of it all.'

'Doesn't Helen want children?'

Raymond's face emptied. 'I hope not.' Then, 'I don't know what anyone wants anymore.'

Alice was fed up. Two weeks at Rosie's while Crispin slid from roseola infantum to earache to overall beastliness, coupled with the knowledge that her immersion heater wasn't working, had left her ill-prepared for Ginny's phone call.

Huddled over her Welsh rarebit, she chewed ruefully at the bubbling crust. She was surprised. Ashamed of her failure to anticipate the crisis, guiltily she reviewed her son's recent behaviour, searching in his grumbling sarcasm for the signs which she, of all people, should have recognised.

But, then, he had always been short with her. He had always been short with Ginny. Could anyone have foreseen his outburst over the wine vinegar as a deliberate pointer to adultery? Hadn't he said roughly the same five years ago about a packet of Weetabix? Ginny was pregnant two months later.

Raymond, that most predictable of sons, had fooled them all. Ginny hadn't said a lot. It was difficult to tell if she wasn't, perhaps, relieved. She'd been bored out of her mind for months – years, really. That was why she'd found her alternative, whoever he was. It was probably all for the best.

There was small danger of her losing her grandchildren, since Ginny was constantly in need of babysitters, and, anyway, they were friends. But what about Lizzie and Matthew? Did they know, or had Ginny just said Daddy was away on business?

Should she ring Raymond or wait till he contacted her?

Would she have to meet Helen?

What if she liked her?

Who was going to mend the immersion?

Alice ate a raspberry sundae and retired to bed unbathed.

'Here we are,' Ginny placed the real coffee on a tray and carried it to the table. 'Do sit down, Delia. You're making me nervous.'

Delia, happy in this knowledge, dusted a chair with a newspaper and laid the *Oklahoma* scores reverently across it.

'It's just what you need. Activity. The last thing you want is to sit here and brood. Get out. Meet fresh people. Prove to yourself you're not just a relic. You can sew, can't you?'

'Not really,' Ginny demurred.

'Nonsense. Of course you can. Anyone can sew. Remember those dungarees you made for Matthew.' Delia's voice died away as she recalled them herself.

'Well, anyway, you can carry a spear. Bulk out the backline. The important thing is to re-establish yourself as an entity. You're a whole person now, not just half a one.'

Ginny wondered if bulking out the backline would provide the necessary proof of this.

'I didn't know they had spears in *Oklahoma*.'

'Well, pitchforks, whatever.'

'But Delia, I can't sing a note.'

'Nonsense, of course you can. Or if not, mime. Really, Ginny, I think you should try to be more positive. It happens to us all, you know, one time or another.'

Ginny's eyebrows rose. 'I didn't realise you and Richard. . .'

'Not Richard and me. Good God no. But masses of couples split up nowadays, you know. One in three marriages is headed for disaster.'

'Perhaps my next two will prove more satisfactory.'

Delia sniffed. 'The point is we need more people. Come along on Thursday night. You won't have to audition. I'll just tell Edward you're for the chorus. Don't worry. It'll do you the world of good. They're doing *West Side Story* next year.'

Delia rose from the couch, extricated her bag and swept towards the door.

Ginny was trailing despondently behind when Delia swooped round in a moment of unbargained for sorority. Clutching Ginny's arm as one bent on two submissions, she hissed, 'I do feel for you, you know. And the children, of course. And Matthew so thin.' She gazed darkly into Ginny's bewildered eyes, then turned and flowed down the steps to her Honda.

She hadn't meant to tell Mitchell.

Now he was here. In their house. Her house now, she supposed.

'Are you saving these for something?'

Mitchell had removed the papers from two of the chairs and was stacking them methodically by the Wendy house.

'What?'

'The newspapers.'

'What's the point of saving newspapers?'

'Who knows, if you don't?'

'The dustmen won't take them.'

'Why not?'

'They're not rubbish.'

'Wrap a kipper in them.'

'You'd need more than one.'

'Never heard of miracles?'

'I don't want to be stuck with five thousand kippers in a second-hand freezer.'

'No sense of proportion, that's your trouble.'

'No sense at all, really.'

'When are the children coming back?'

'Tomorrow teatime.'

'Pity.'

'Why?'

'We could've gone down the baths in the morning. They shut at twelve.'

'Pity.'

Ginny slid off the arm of the chair, which she had been listlessly dabbing with vinegar.

'Did it work?'

'What?'

'The vinegar?'

'If you mean "Does the chair smell like a fish shop?" Yes.'

'Did it move the ink?'

'It seems to be spreading, certainly.'

'Are you mad at me?'

'Why should I be?'

'I don't know. Unless I don't go with your furniture.'

'You more or less outnumber it.'

'Has he taken a lot, then?'

'There wasn't a lot to take. No, curse him, he's left all the good bits and taken all the comfortable ones.'

'Do you want to talk about it?'

'Well, there was a brown sofa with a dog embroidered on the middle cushion – strangely hideous, but very good for playing Superman. . .'

Mitchell got up. 'I'm going.'

'I seem to have this effect on people,' said Ginny, and started to cry.

Mitchell regarded her for a moment, then produced a handkerchief.

'It's not nice for you. Me being here. It's not what we intended.'

'It is nice,' Ginny moaned. 'If you go I'll have no one to loathe.'

Mitchell smiled. 'I might as well make it worth your while, then. Did he leave the deck chairs?'

'Oh no,' said Ginny. 'Never again.'

'It was wonderful.'

'It was wonderful for you. You were on top.'

Mitchell pondered. 'I don't think it would work the other way round.'

'Spoken like a coward. Fetch the white feathers.'

Mitchell's face lit up. 'Now that *is* a good idea.'

Mr Rolfe dunked his gingernut.

'You see, I could do it. I could do it for you easy. But I don't want to.'

Alice waited enquiringly.

'The reason I don't want to is, if I do it now, in six months' time I'll have to do it again.'

Again Alice waited.

'And you wouldn't want that.'

'No,' said Alice. 'I wouldn't.'

'No,' said Mr Rolfe. 'I didn't think you would.'

There was a pause.

'Mightn't it be possible,' queried Alice, 'to do it in such a way that it might last a little longer than six months?'

A hiss escaped from Mr Rolfe as he attempted to whistle.

'I can't see it, Mrs J. mum, dearie. You see, the wiring's gone. Had it. I can patch it up all right. I can do that for you. But it won't last. It needs replacing, you see.'

'And you can't replace it?'

'Oh, I can replace it. I can do that all right.'

'But?'

'Were you wanting it replaced, then?'

'Mr Rolfe. It is November. I have no hot water. I do not wish to wait till May for a bath. If you know of a way to prevent this, I implore you to confide in me.'

Mr Rolfe drank deep and gazed meaningfully at the teapot.

'You want it replaced then?'

'When could you do it?'

Another hiss.

'I'm not sure.'

'I appreciate this must be your busy time. . .'

'You see it's my busy time just now.'

'I feared as much.'

'I've got a lot on.'

'I can see I've been wasting your time. I'll have to find someone else.'

'Hold on now, Mrs J. mum, dear, I'm not saying I couldn't squeeze you in.'

'When?'

Alice put the kettle on.

'Well, I won't say no to another cup if you're having one yourself.'

'I'm not. This water is for my personal laundry.'

Mr Rolfe returned at five o'clock and left about seven, the richer by £22 – which Alice accounted money well spent, despite having forgotten to buy more Radox.

Matthew trickled the syrup over his Shreddies.

'When's Daddy coming home?'

'He's very busy just now, darling.'

'He hasn't had his breakfast.'

'He's having it somewhere else.'

'At work?'

'I don't know. Probably.'

'How can he work if he's eating his toast?'

'How can you chatter if you're eating your cereal?'

'Doesn't Daddy live here now?'

Ginny stirred her sugarless tea. 'Daddy had to go away for a while.'

'To Abroad?'

'No, not abroad.'

'Has he gone to see Grammar?'

'Matthew, Daddy's gone to stay with a friend.'

'Why didn't you go?'

'I have to look after you and Lizzie.'

'We could all go. Why didn't we all go?'

Ginny's mind thrashed about for an answer. 'You'd miss your swimming lesson.'

'I don't mind. I don't like them.'

Tears of injustice swamped her eyes. 'You're an ungrateful little swine.'

Matthew's howl of mortification pursued her up the stairs: 'I want Daddy. I'm going to tell him what you said. You're not my best-ever friend anymore.'

I can't keep crying, thought Ginny, eyeing her bloated visage. It's not even as though I miss him. I'm crying for them because they do.

The memory of Lizzie clunking round the house chanting

'Dada, Dada, Daddeee' was too much. She crumpled up beside the chair and bellowed with misery.

A small velvet hand gripped her elbow.

'It's all right, Mummy. You are my best-ever friend, really. Daddy's just my second best.'

Eileen sat up suddenly.

Gerry opened one eye. 'What's the matter?'

'Nothing. I thought I heard someone.'

'It'll be next door. The walls are like paper here.' Eileen sat for a moment listening, then shivered and lay down.

Gerry's arm reached across her. 'You're freezing. I'll have to do something about that.'

'Like what?'

'Like this.'

Eileen squealed coyly as Gerry engulfed her. 'I must go home. It's nearly four o'clock.'

'What's the rush?'

'I want to . . . I've got to start the meal.'

'You can always have fish and chips.'

Eileen looked genuinely surprised. 'It's not Friday.'

'Are you a Catholic, then?'

'No, why?'

'I thought only Catholics had fish on Friday.'

'Do they? No, well, I usually have my practice on Fridays, or else I go down to Marion's, so I can't be bothered cooking.'

'Doesn't hubby object?'

'He likes fish and chips. Anyway, he's usually late on Fridays. Extra class.'

'What a busy life you lead, little Eileen.'

'Not so much of the little.'

'You are little. I like little womn. So long as they're not too little.' He bent over and kissed her breasts.

Eileen wriggled voluptuously. 'I must go home.'

'Who's stopping you?'

'You are.'

'No I'm not. Off you go. Don't forget your knickers.'

Eileen didn't altogether enjoy this line of banter, but she smiled and began to gather her clothes.

'What're you doing tomorrow?'

'When?'

'Evening, of course.'

'Oh, we're going to see my mum. I promised Jeanette we'd go over.'

'Pity. There's a great band at the Fox. Thought you might fancy it.'

'Sorry.'

Gerry shrugged. 'Not to worry.'

'Shall I ring you?'

'Yes, do that, darling.' Gerry reached for her hand and pulled her down beside him. He kissed her rather perfunctorily. 'See you, Eileen,' he said and lay back on the pillows, his hands behind his head.

'Right,' said Eileen a little unsteadily.

She opened the bedroom door and went through to the lounge-diner. Sue was sitting on the sofa, scrutinising *Nineteen*.

'Oh, hallo, Eileen,' she said. 'Going to the practice on Monday?'

'I think so,' stuttered Eileen and, seizing her raincoat, fled in search of a number twelve bus.

Raymond seemed incapable of sitting down.

Helen glanced at him with growing irritation as he prowled from window to table to bookcase, flicking lamp switches and rearranging condiments.

The chops spattered in the grill-pan as she stirred the Béchemel sauce. Fleetingly she wondered if she should have peeled the new potatoes, then, noticing Raymond turn the television on and off for the third time, she grimly sliced the tomatoes and hurled them into the lamb's heart salad.

Raymond sidled into the kitchen and stood. 'Anything I can do?'

'No thanks. It won't be long.'

Raymond remained in the arch. 'Smells good.'

'Good.'

'Shall I turn those chops?'

'I've done it.'

'I like them brown.'

'Darling, why don't you sit down? It'll be ready in ten ticks.'

'Can't I carry something through for you?'

'There's nothing to carry. Oh, take the salad, would you, darling?'

The sauce had begun to boil.

Raymond resumed his place. 'I think those chops might be done.'

'I know they're done.' Helen seized the pan and heaved it on to the draining board. Boiling fat shrapnelled her.

'Did you burn yourself?' Raymond advanced solicitously.

'Not much.' Her blouse was ruined. 'Could you pass me a fork?'

'A fork. Yes. Where are they?'

'In the drawer by the sink.'

'This one?'

'Yes.'

'A big one?'

'I don't mind. Just a fork.'

Raymond passed her a fish knife.

Helen swiped the chops onto the platter and went to rescue her sauce, which was frothing on the simmer plate.

'I must say this looks scrumptious.'

Raymond poured the too good wine.

'Our first dinner,' proffered Helen shyly. Raymond looked surprised.

'I mean, at home.' The words slithered away.

Now they were both embarrassed.

Raymond crunched his cutlets. 'Where did you learn to cook?'

'At school.'

'I love the sauce.'

'Thank you.'

Helen had finished her wine.

Raymond refilled her glass.

The baked Alaska had leaked.

Helen giggled immoderately.

Raymond was disappointed. He loved puddings.

'I expect it will taste the same.'

'How can it? The meringue's stuck to the oven.'

Helen poured herself some more wine. Her forehead shone in the candlelight.

Why does she wear so much make-up? Raymond pondered. She's only twenty-three.

'Aren't you having any?' Helen pointed to the bottle with her spoon.

'In a minute, perhaps.'

'Why are you staring at me?'

Raymond hesitated. A moment too long. 'I'm looking at you.'

Helen reached out for his hand. He gave it to her.

A moment too late.

Ginny huddled in the auditorium.

Canvas chairs cringed against the lobelia walls, which still harboured the tattered vestiges of the Age Concern Christmas Bonanza. Fat, grumbling pipes lined the hall, their complaints periodically erupting into a series of pistol-like cracks as the heating rose to its prescribed eleven Celsius, then subsiding again as someone ran the hot water tap. Two middle-aged men in golf sweaters with logos loped to and fro, one nursing a steel tape measure and the other a piece of yellow chalk, were ostensibly engaged in seat allocation. It was hard to believe from their conversation that a degree in civil engineering was not a requisite qualification for the task.

'How many have we got on the mayor's side, then?'

'Sixteen.'

'So that's...' fingers stabbed at the air.

'... seven, right of the gangway.'

'Eight, surely?'

More stabbing.

'Seven.'

'You're right.'

'Nineteen rows of thirty-three. That's ... four hundred and thirty-seven, if I'm not mistaken.'

The other man conceded this figure.

'What about wheelchairs?'

'Christ, I'd forgotten them. Can't they go down the sides?' Sharp intake of breath.

'Fire regulations, Leo, my cocker. No chance.'

'What to do, then?'

'Better talk to Edward. Better still, Judith.'

'Right.'

Leo went in search of Judith, who, it was rumoured, was in the kitchen, ironing the haystack.

'What am I doing here?' Ginny pondered forlornly, as she thumbed through her *Observer*.

'What are you doing here?'

She looked up.

Peter Bailey, Emma's husband, peered down at her.

Ginny grimaced. 'I might ask you the same question.'

'I've brought some tablecloths Delia made Emma sew for the barn dance.'

'She got off very lightly.'

'You're not in it, are you?' asked Peter in grim alarm.

Ginny shrugged defensively.

'Oh, Ginny.' Peter was trying not to laugh. 'No wonder Emma couldn't get you on the phone.'

'There are some things one doesn't like to talk about.'

'Well, don't monopolise them.'

Ginny spluttered with laughter. 'Promise not to tell Emma.'

'You couldn't do that to me.'

'Well, *only* Emma, then.'

'Of course.'

He kissed her lightly on the forehead, and retreated through the coils of unnecessary cable and rubicund flats depicting summer in the Midwest.

Ginny scoured her bag for rolls.

She found them lurking, cressless, underneath her Tupperware make-up box. Morosely she sank her teeth into the pappy bread and tried to absorb Sue Arnold's views on au pairs. Leo and his crony were once more fumbling with the tape measure. Ginny suspected that they wanted her to move, so kept her eyes firmly lowered.

'If you could give me a couple in Row G,' Leo mooted, 'I think I can shake it.'

'G? I can let you have some in H. How would that suit you?'

'Hmm. H? Yes, that should be all right. Hang on, though,

what about the pillar? No, that'll be obstructed view. Can't have that for the wheelchairs. What's wrong with G? I only need a couple.'

'It's right by the exit,' explained Leo. 'What if there's a fire?'

'Oh, right. Hadn't thought of that.'

'Right. Thinking caps again.'

'Perhaps we should have a word with Judith?'

'Good idea.'

This time they both went.

'Has anyone seen Katherine?'

A limp silvern figure was roaming the forestage, watery eyes shielded from the glare of three footlights which Ronnie, the electrician, had at last managed to coax into operation. It gazed sorrowfully into the auditorium.

'Leo, is that you?'

'Yes, Edward. I'm just sorting out the seating.'

'Jolly good. Haven't seen Katherine, have you?'

'She was at rehearsal on Friday.'

Edward quivered. 'Yes, I remember that, Leo. I took it. I meant this morning.'

'Ah. Now you mention it, I don't think I have.'

'I say, Edward, how do you feel about the wheelchairs going in the circle?'

Edward gazed disbelievingly into the darkness, then with a resigned shudder swivelled on his heels and retreated to the wings.

'Whatever. . .' floated gossamer-like through the hall.

Leo turned triumphantly to Robert. 'There. That's the answer. Put them in the circle.'

Ginny wondered if it mattered that there was no lift.

'Hard at it, that's what I like to see.'

Katherine, in a mushroom cloud of patchouli, clicked across the hall, her hennaed pony tail swinging viciously against the mohair bolero bobbing above her sateen ski pants. The height of her stilettos suggested an unspoken desire to fall nose first over a cliff.

'Edward was looking for you,' Robert informed her. 'He looked a bit fraught.'

'Tell me news, honey,' flipped Katherine and rotated towards the kitchen.

'How's the voice, Katherine?' asked a solicitous choreen.

Katherine's hand sought her throat, Callas-like. 'Murder, darling,' she throbbed. 'I've been inhaling all night.'

'You have to be so careful' said the other. 'There's a lot of it about.'

'And she's tried most of it,' muttered Ronnie, who was a real electrician and consequently tolerated.

Ginny sniggered and poured herself some coffee.

'What's that you're drinking?' asked Ronnie.

'Coffee. Do you want some?'

'Wouldn't mind.'

Ginny filled the second cup and handed it to him. 'There's no sugar, I'm afraid.'

'Don't take it, thanks.' Ronnie supped deep. 'That's real coffee.'

'I thought I might need a stimulant.'

'You weren't in the last one, were you?'

'No.'

'I tell you, this is nothing. Nothing, compared to that.' Another gulp.

'Bloody *Irma La Douce*. You should've seen it. Fourteen poofters chasing Margie Etherington round a camp bed. Tell you something, I wouldn't want to meet her on a dark night in Brixton.

'She's got a lovely voice,' said Ginny without conviction.

'You need more than that to be a tart,' decreed Ronnie. 'Fancy a drink?'

'What's the time?'

'Ten past twelve.'

'They might want to get started. It's nearly an hour till lunch.'

'You are new, aren't you?' said Ronnie. 'Come one.'

The pub was filling up by the time Ronnie had smuggled Ginny past Leo and Robert, who, having exhausted their usefulness front of house, had now positioned themselves by the main exit and were interrogating would-be escapees with a ferocity few would have accorded them.

'What do you mean, "Just a breath of fresh air"?' Ginny heard Leo bark as she crept through the drapes, blindly trusting herself to Ronnie's experience in these matters. He had, he assured her, 'done two episodes of "Colditz", so this is nothing, love'. Nevertheless, Ginny felt her heart stop as Delia's voice cracked out above her head. They were crouched in the prompt box, waiting for a passing flat behind which to make their run. It came, and Ginny, now thoroughly infected with Ronnie's POW zeal, fled after him into the street and round the corner to the Lemon Tree.

'Better try the Queen's Head,' Ronnie decided when they had got their breath back. 'Bit risky in here. Wouldn't put it past those two Brownies to come snooping.' Ginny hastily agreed and together they scurried along the street to the next pub.

'Thank Christ for that,' puffed Ronnie as they slumped into the corner seat. 'What are you having?'

'Two brandies and a pint of Guinness.'

'Right.'

'Not really,' Ginny laughingly restrained him. 'I'll have a white wine, please. Dry.'

'Thank Christ for that,' said Ronnie again. 'I've only got a tenner.'

'Here, let me get them. I've got some money.'

'Didn't mean that. You get the next lot. Want a pie?'

'No, thanks.'

Ronnie rose and struggled to the bar, returning with their drinks and a shrivelled clod of pastry. They both drank deep.

'I feel like an escaped convict,' said Ginny, 'I daren't look anyone in the eyes, in case they recognise me and send for Leo.'

'Why did you join?' asked Ronnie.

'I didn't join. I was commandeered.'

'Delia Crabourne?'

'Delia Crabourne.'

'She's something else, that one. My Jean, she used to do the refreshments, come home in tears during the last one. She's only gone and told her she can't boil a kettle.'

'No!'

'She bloody has. Said there'd been complaints about the coffee – too weak or summat. Jean says they shouldn't buy el cheapo coffee, then, and next thing is she's telling everyone my Jean's not fit to be in charge. I ask you.'

'What did you do?'

'I'll tell you what I did.' Ronnie quaffed his beer. 'I go in next night, I unplug the urn – full of boiling water it is – and I go round to the storeroom where her ladyship is counting the teabags, and I says to her, "Mrs Crabourne," I says, "I believe you've got complaints about how my Jean is running the refreshment bar?" '

' "Oh, Mr Clarkson," she says, "You've got it all wrong." ' ' "No," I says, "it's not me what's got it wrong, It's you. Now, here's the water," I says, and I dump it on the table, right in the middle of the fig rolls, I grab a jar of coffee off the shelf – great big things, you know – and I empty the whole bleedin' lot in the urn, then I pick up a paintbrush what's on the floor there, and I stir it all up. "There," I says, "I've made the coffee. I hope it's to your liking. You'll have to excuse me now, I've got some lights to set," and I leaves her to it. Just before the interval it was.'

Ginny screeched with laughter. 'I can just see her face. What happened?'

'Oh, they had to cancel the coffee that evening. And the tea. You know how them granules stick. Bloody urn looked like someone'd been making jam in it. She never bothered my Jean again, though.'

Ginny gazed ruefully at her empty glass. 'I wish someone'd stick up for me like that. My round.'

Ronnie's tenner coupled with Ginny's five pounds thirty

saw them cheerfully through the lunch-hour opening, each meticulously paying their way until they lost track when Ginny was sent in search of crisps and came back with two glasses of Malibu. This they jointly pronounced disgusting, but decided to drink anyway, on the grounds that it was probably full of protein.

'Time, gentlemen, please.'

'That's the third time he's said that,' Ginny drawled, quite incapable of making the connection between the request and herself.

'I think he wants us to go,' Ronnie acknowledged.

'*Us?*' snorted Ginny. 'Why *us?* What have *we* done?' She clambered unsteadily to her feet and weaved towards the bar. Ronnie, who, though very well oiled, was not noticeably the worse for wear, followed her rather like a parent watching his toddler take her first steps.

'Excuse me.' Ginny addressed her remarks to the back of the barman's neck. 'But I heard that.' The amiable Irishman turned round and smiled at her disarmingly. 'I'm very glad. To tell the truth, I was getting tired of saying it.'

'It wasn't very nice.' Ginny sat down suddenly on the edge of a table, effectively removing her from the man's eyeline. Assuming that she had collapsed, he put down the glass he had been polishing and peered anxiously over the top of the counter. Ronnie winked at him, hauled Ginny up and draped her arm round his neck, his own supporting her firmly round the waist. Ginny giggled. 'Where are we going now?'

'Back to the lion's den. You can have a nice sleep in the dressing room. Soon be time to go home.'

'Don't want to go back there.' Ginny pouted.

'Home?'

'No, lion's den. Don't like lions. Don't like Leo.' Her free hand pounded Ronnie's chest as she strove to impart the joke that was now convulsing her whole body. 'D'you get it?' she spluttered. 'Lions . . . Leo . . . Leo the lion.'

'That's very good,' said Ronnie kindly and bundled her

out of the pub into the cold Sunday air, and back to St Mark's church hall.

'I think she should be taken home straight away', said Delia. 'She's no good to us like that and poor Edward has enough problems without a drunken cowgirl.'

A muffled rendition of 'I'm just a girl who can't say no' issued from the kitchen, where Ginny was refusing Nescafé.

Judith had forsaken her haystack and was hovering awkwardly beside the wrathful Delia.

'The trouble is it's the dress at four o'clock. We really need everyone there. Edward's very particular about it.'

Delia withered her. 'Listen to her, Judith. Do you seriously think she'll prove an asset to the production as she is?'

Judith's mouth worked in several directions, but since no sound came out Delia took it that her point had been made.

'Well, I can't do it. I've got to see to the programmes. You'd better take her.'

A strange rattle issued from Judith's throat.

'Oh, very well. I'll find someone else.'

'Perhaps Ronnie. . .'

'Ronnie? Why Ronnie?'

'Well, er, she was with Ronnie in the pub, I think. She might like to go with him.'

'Judith, the state Ginny Jeavons is in, I imagine she'd like to go with anyone. We can't possibly let Ronnie go. We need him for the fit-up.'

'I could ask Robert. Or Leo. I think Leo's free.'

'Right. Find Leo. Send him to me in the kitchen.' Delia strode to the appointed rendezvous.

The sight of Ginny athwart the ironing board, swirling a canvas sheepdog and striving ineffectually for high C, gave her a second's pause, but Delia was not easily dismayed.

'Now, Ginny, come and put your coat on. Leo's going to give you a lift home.'

' "Don't throw bouquets at me" ', trilled the inebriate.

'Where are your things? Is this your bag?'

' "Don't laugh at my jokes too much".' Ginny hinted at pathos.

'Are you going to have some of this coffee Eleanor's so kindly made for you? I think it might be a good idea.'

' "People will say we're in love".' This to Leo, whose nervous demeanour was more suited to the presence of an imperial corpse.

Ginny pirouetted unsteadily across the floor.

' "Oooooh the cowman and the farmer should be friends".' Leo tried unsuccessfully to extricate himself from a friendship more intimate than he would have wished.

'Ginny.' Delia's voice was like thunder. 'Pull yourself together. We are waiting to begin the dress rehearsal. Edward is very pressed for time.'

'He's very pressed for hair, too,' giggled Ginny. 'And talent.'

'Oh, for God's sake,' drawled Katherine, who resented such attention being focused on an extra.

Ginny peeled herself cautiously from Leo's lapels and confronted the unfortunate contralto.

'Not so pressed', the sheepdog swirled menacingly, 'as certain persons, members of the honable, honourabable cast who should be nameless, if they had half as much sense as they've got bad breath.'

With this she swivelled inconclusively and tottered towards the hall.

'I'll take you in the wings again, Katherine,' crashed upon the gentrified ears of the Acton Hill Operatics, as Ginny weaved towards the broom cupboard, the fridge-freezer and, eventually, the door.

'Mummy isn't very well.' Matthew clamped the mouthpiece to his chest and addressed his remarks to the television.

'Darling, can you speak a bit louder? I can't quite hear you.'

'Mummy isn't very well.'

'Who is it, Matthew?'

The lettuce face of Ginny peered through the door.

'Oh, Mummy, you should be lying down,' bossed Matthew.

Ginny reeled at the onslaught. 'Yes, I know, darling, but who is it? Shall I have a word?'

'It's Grammar. I told her you're not very well. She says you're all right but I said you're not.'

'Let me have a word, darling.' Ginny swayed towards the phone and concertinaed over it.

'Alice?'

'Yes.'

'Thank God.'

'What's happened?'

'I'm drunk.'

'So?'

'I'm not drunk anymore. I'm *ill*.'

'Do you want me to come over?'

'No. No, of course not.'

'I could, you know, Ginny. It wouldn't take long. I could put them to bed for you.'

'Oh, Alice, I wouldn't dream of it. It would be an implosish. . .un.'

'I'll see you in an hour,' said Alice.

'Is Mummy going to Devon, Grammar?'

'I don't think so, darling. She's going to bed. She doesn't feel very well.'

'I mean when she dies. Will she go to Devon then?'

'Gracious, darling, I don't know. Does she want to?'

'Well, all the good mummies go to Devon, don't they? To be with Jesus.'

'Oh. That Devon. Yes, I expect so. Why, darling?'

'Mummy says she's dying. Who's going to take care of me and Lizzie then? Are you going to? Or is Daddy coming back?'

Alice winced. 'I think Mummy was just joking, darling. She isn't really going to die. Not for a long time.'

'Not for hundreds of years?'

'Something like that.'

'When will you die, Grammar? You're very old, aren't you?'

'Yes. I suppose I am.'

'Hundreds of years?'

'Not quite.'

'Mummy. . .' Matthew hurtled gleefully up the stairs. 'Grammar's hundreds of years old and she's going to live in Devon when she dies.'

'Really, darling?' Ginny intoned balefully. 'How lovely.'

'I don't see why you have to phone her so often.' Helen dragged her voice back from the precipice of a whine. 'I do understand that you have to keep in touch. About the children and everything. I don't mean to moan. Gosh, I'm turning into a nag already.' She smiled uncertainly and topped up his Campari.

It tasted of medicated shampoo. Or what he assumed it to taste of. Helen liked it and seemed to think he must, too. He really must get down to his wine merchant. He had to stop her buying Niersteiner in the lunch hour. He could always have a whisky, but then he would get sentimental and start talking about the children, which wasn't very nice for Helen. Poor girl. She tried so hard to please him. He was very fond of her, of course, and immensely flattered by her devotion, but sometimes there did seem to be something missing.

The biting edge.

Cow though Ginny undoubtedly was, she did make him laugh sometimes. Not in a middle-aged way as he did with Helen, gently mocking her earnestness, but with the open-hearted malice they had shared, at least in the first years of their marriage.

Ginny had never lost it.

Nor had he. Or had he?

No, of course he hadn't.

Obviously he had to temper it a bit at JCV. But at home? At home.

'When is Daddy coming home?'

Alice peeled Lizzie from the witch's hat and strapped her ramrod torso into the buggy.

'Where's your bike, darling? You mustn't keep leaving it or someone beastly might take it away.'

'A burglar?'

'Yes.'

'Will a policeman shoot him?'

'He might not be able to find him. Or your bike.'

'When he does, will he shoot him?'

'I don't think so, Matthew.'

'Why not?'

'Because policeman don't shoot people for stealing things.'

'Even if they're very horrid?'

'No. They send them to prison usually.'

'Would the burglar ride my bike in prison?'

'Oh, no. The policeman would give it back to you, if he found it. But the burglar might have sold it to someone else.'

'Why?'

'For money.'

'How much money?'

'I don't know, darling. Quite a lot.'

'Nine thousand pounds?'

'Something like that.'

Matthew ruminated, then walked slowly to where his Boxer sprawled against the slide.

'Grammar. . .'

'Yes, darling.'

'Would you like to buy my bike?'

'But where is he?' Eileen gazed beseechingly into Susan's diminutive eyes.

'God knows,' shrugged Susan. 'He went on a bender with Gordon on Friday night and I haven't seen either of them since. He was meant to be going to Crawleys Folk Night on Sunday, too. I'm really pissed off with that Gordon. And he's got dandruff.'

'Didn't he say anything? I mean, a message or something?' Susan peered gloomily at Eileen.

'What sort of message?'

The blood swooped up from Eileen's toes. She bit her cheeks and stared desperately at the coffee table.

'Oh, I dunno. I thought he was going to ring me, about going to a jazz concert, he said.'

'Doesn't your Dave mind? You kicking around with Gerry, I mean.'

'He doesn't like jazz.'

'All the same. We could've all gone. Made it a foursome.' If Eileen had had any doubts as to the advantages of Susan's friendship, she now perceived them to be valid.

'Well,' she murmured lamely, 'I'd better get off home. Marion and Jeff are coming round for their tea.'

Susan's lips split malevolently. 'Oh, that's nice. What are you giving them?'

'I've got a tin of salmon,' Eileen revealed. 'To tell the truth, I wish they weren't. I'm feeling a bit . . . you know.'

Susan's eyebrows arched enquiringly. 'What?'

'Oh, nothing really. You know. . . sick.'

Ginny and Alice sat side by side, fingers wrapped round their mulled wine.

'What are you thinking of doing?'

'I don't know. A shop, I suppose. It would have to be part-time.'

'What about an office?'

Ginny's face contorted. 'You know my typing. Anyway, I'd go mad. No one ever opens the windows. Do you remember that time? No, it was before I knew Raymond. I worked at the Pay Board for three weeks, when they were winding it up. I used to sit in a hermetically sealed locker room with two phones, opposite a woman called Doris with two more. Every time one of mine rang I had to ask the name and company of the caller, the nature of the query and the number of employees. Armed with this information, I would reply "Thank you very much, sir. Unfortunately this is not my department, but I can give you the number of someone who will be able to help you." I would then give him a completely different number and two minutes later Doris's phone would ring and the poor sod would have to go through it all again for her. The climax came when she would say, in a very high-pitched voice, "Could you possibly put this in writing, sir. Then we can deal with it immediately." '

'What sort of a shop?'

'Doesn't really matter. Ironmongers, butchers, florist.'

Alice's eyes rolled upwards.

'I like flowers.' Ginny murmured defensively.

'Pity it's not mutual.' Alice gazed sternly at the dying spider plants.

'Anyway there's not much round here. I'd have to take what's going.'

'Ginny.' Alice was embarrassed. 'Is Raymond keeping you short?'

'Oh, God, no.' Ginny almost laughed. 'No, he's pouring money over us. Christ knows what he and Helen are living on. Poor girl's probably paying all the bills as well as servicing him.'

There was a silence.

'Are you very sad about it?'

'I don't know. I was rather pleased to start with. Once I'd got over the shock. Everyone was so cheerful. I got invited out, I got drunk and I still got asked back. Nobody seemed to mind what I did. I think that's what I miss most. Nobody minding. Do you think there's too much ginger in this?'

'I like the ginger. It warms me up.'

'Speaking of which – how's your boiler?'

'The immersion?'

'Yes.'

'Fine. If I don't use it too often.'

'How much is too often?'

'Once a day.'

'Oh, Alice, that's awful. You must get it done properly. What'll happen if we have a cold spell?'

'I shall knit myself a cardigan.'

'You'd be better off knitting a jacket for the boiler. You must be losing a fortune through it.'

'I expect so.'

'I'll find someone to have a look at it for you.'

'I've had someone.'

'A proper plumber. Then I'll take the blame if it still isn't fixed.'

'It's very sweet of you, Ginny, but honestly I don't think it's necessary.'

'A proper plumber is what you need, and a proper plumber is what you're going to get.'

Alice sighed.

'Where shall we have lunch?'

'McDonalds.'

Raymond had anticipated more room for manoeuvre.

'What about somewhere Italian? Then you could have a pizza or some spaghetti?'

'I want to go to McDonalds.'

'What about Lizzie, though? She doesn't like hamburgers.'

'She doesn't like spaghetti.'

'Well she could have an ice cream.'

'She can have one at McDonalds.'

Raymond drew a breath and thought on Helen's advice: Don't try and make them do what you want.

'All right. McDonalds it is.'

Matthew led the way, weaving in and out amongst trundling family outings and torpid OAPs, till his father lost sight of him as he dribbled the ecstatic Lizzie through the ubiquitous cluster of shops. When he finally caught up, it was to be faced by a grief-stricken Matthew.

'What on earth's the matter? And please don't keep running off like that. I thought I'd lost you.'

Raymond pushed open the door of McDonalds, and found himself eyeball to eyeball with a teenaged girl in the obligatory brown pyjamas.

'Egg muffins and shakes only,' she intoned.

Raymond was unmoved. Turning to Matthew, he beckoned with his head. Matthew's face grew dark with anguish.

'Daddy,' he hopped from foot to foot. 'They've got no *chips*.'

'Well, never mind,' said Raymond, a trifle impatiently. 'Have something else.'

'I need *chips*.' The hopping was extremely rapid.

'You need a pee, by the look of you. Come on in, and stop being so daft.'

This was too much for Matthew, who dissolved into tears but stood his ground. 'You said I could have chips.'

Exasperated, Raymond rounded on the waitress. 'You've got chips,' he uttered menacingly. 'Haven't you?'

'Egg muffins and shakes only,' returned the stoic female.

'What kind of a place is this?' Raymond croaked with unaccustomed vehemence. 'Why haven't you got chips? What have you done with them?'

'The fryer's bust.'

'Well, it's a bloody disgrace. Come on, Matthew, we'll go somewhere else.'

Matthew, somewhat encouraged by the outlandish behaviour of his father, and basking in the respectful glances of such customers as had pronounced themselves content with eggburgers, clasped his father's hand firmly, and led the way out on to the broad pavement.

It was at this point that Raymond discovered Lizzie gone. Wildly he cast around for her.

'Stay here with the buggy, Matthew. Don't dare move. I'll be back in two ticks.'

With this, Raymond plunged into the King's Mall, only to return minutes later, still minus his daughter.

Matthew had not moved, and was eating a Farley's rusk he had found gently rotting in the pocket of the pushchair.

'Where did you go, Daddy?'

'I'm looking for Lizzie. If she runs into the road. . .'

'Lizzie's in there.'

'In where?'

Matthew's eyes were orbs of astonishment. 'In there. In McDonalds.'

Raymond spun round to be confronted once more by the beaming face of Lizzie, one hand clasping a bunch of multi-coloured straws, the other firmly implanted in that of the derided waitress.

Maroon beneath his weekend bristles, Raymond reclaimed

the prodigal and frogmarched the protesting pair to Hosteria Luigi.

'What's the matter now?' Raymond watched Matthew dipping disconsolately into his tomato and sorrel soup. 'I thought you liked tomato soup.'

'I've gone off it.'

'Well, eat your roll.'

'What's that?'

'Smoked trout.'

Raymond tried ineffectually to transport the flaking fillet to his mouth. Again Lizzie's gaping gums bore down upon his fork, scattering the morsel before Raymond's famished lips could grasp it.

'Oh, for God's sake, Lizzie, you can't have it all. Let Daddy have a bit, there's a good girl.'

Lizzie, unmoved by this exhortation, snuggled closer, preparatory to launching herself at the Barolo.

'Can I have some Coke, Daddy.'

'I don't think they have it.'

'You've got some.'

'This isn't Coke. It's wine. You wouldn't like it.'

'I would. I like wine.'

'Since when?'

'Since always. When I was in Mummy's tummy.'

'You wouldn't like this. Drink your orange.'

'I would. I've gone off orange.'

'Well, try it then. I bet you don't like it.'

Matthew drank deep.

'Here, that's enough. You'll fall asleep.'

'Does wine make you sleepy?'

'Sometimes.'

'Are you sleepy?'

'No, but I'm bigger than you. It doesn't affect me the same way.'

'Not even if you drank a hundred thousands of it?'

'That might make me a bit sleepy.'

Matthew's spaghetti arrived, and a fresh supply of bread-sticks, since Lizzie had dropped most of them in the water jug. Raymond gave her a roll, which she lovingly crumbled into his pullover.

He decided to forget the trout and wait for his *scaloppine*. Matthew swivelled his pasta round the plate like a gyroscope. Raymond bore it as long as his echoing stomach could, then snarled: 'Matthew, are you going to eat that spaghetti, or simply play with it? Because if the latter, a box of plasticine would have served as well and cost a lot less.'

The child gazed in bemused sorrow at his father, and Raymond perceived that he had forfeited his effect. Matthew didn't understand.

'Just eat your lunch, there's a good chap. Then we can go to the park.'

'Which park?'

'The one down the road.'

'Ole Pole Park?'

'No, not that one. Ravenscourt. You'll enjoy that, won't you?'

'I don't like parks.'

'Yes, you do,' said Raymond crisply, as his food arrived. Lizzie, who was sleepy, had eased off her attacks marginally, and Raymond was able to replenish his flagging stamina.

Matthew continued to mutilate his lunch to the extent that the waiter enquired 'Eef anysing wass wrong?'

Raymond shook his head helplessly and finished his half carafe. Ice cream was proferred and for a moment it seemed that the meal might yet be a success, but, inevitably, Matthew had gone off strawberry. Minutes later, fists gripping their thin mints, the children were steered back into the daylight, which had intuitively darkened to match Raymond's mood. On to the park, where a prevailing north-easterly cut at them as they swung morosely on the rubber tyres.

'Daddy.'

'Yes, Matthew?'

'Lizzie's done a poo.'

'Are you sure?'

'I can smell her. She's done a poo.'

'All right, all right. I suppose we'd better change her, hadn't we?'

Peering suspiciously into the Mothercare carryall Ginny had thrust at him that morning, Raymond was confronted by nappies, certainly, but what were all the other bits for?

Gingerly he extracted a tube of Drapolene, Babywipes, plastic pants, a polythene bag, and two more Farleys rusks wrapped in Clingfilm.

The problem of where to perform the operation now arose, since the grass was damp, and the men's lavatory hardly seemed appropriate. Raymond settled for a bench, spreading his implements neatly around the edge. One thing he lacked — anaesthetic. Lizzie was not keen to have her nappy changed. In fact, she was ferociously opposed to the idea. Gumboots flailed, arms thrashed, wild and haunting cries emitted from her at regular intervals as she contrived to force her stubby body into an arc of angry vertebrae. Raymond struggled and cursed, watched keenly by his son.

'You haven't wiped her bottom, Daddy. You forgot the cream. She'll have a sore botty now. Mummy doesn't do it like that.'

Had both Raymond's hands not been so amply employed, Matthew's discourse might have ended there. As it was, he was able to chunter on, his advice supremely negative, until his eyes lit upon the crumbled rusks lying now at the edge of the sandpit.

'Can I have one of these, please, Daddy?'

'Have what you like. Just stop talking for a minute, will you?'

'These are my favourite.'

'I thought they were for babies. Give Lizzie one, will you?'

Matthew did so.

'Can we go and look at the ship, please Daddy?'

'What ship?'

'The one in the adventure playground.'

'Where's that?'

'Down the other end. Past the teashop.'

'Yes, all right.'

Twenty minutes later, the rain beginning to fall, they stood gazing up at the fading glory of the wooden galleon *Ravenscourt*, hymn to the skill and efforts of the now disgruntled playleaders. The children grasped their wholefood ice creams at forty p a cone, Matthew having overcome his distaste for strawberry.

Raymond's heart sank as he surveyed the sea of mud estranging them from the noble vessel.

'It's a bit muddy,' he demurred, but Matthew was already halfway across, splattering the slime with a joy equalling London busdrivers after a cloudburst.

Lizzie followed, slithering and plunging, narrowly avoided by the crop of BMX bikes swirling around the swamp.

Raymond swore and made his way after them.

At the side of the ship dangled a rope ladder, up which Matthew swarmed, eyes bright with resolve. Lizzie clung to the bottom, snorting and stamping, and howled so savagely when Matthew disappeared from view, that her ravaged father could do no less than lift her on to it, too. This done, he was also obliged to board.

The rain was reasonably heavy now.

'Come on, Matthew, let's go and get some tea. It's awfully cold on this ship of yours.'

'There's nowhere to land.'

'What about over there, by the slide? Couldn't you weigh anchor, and we could disembark and scout around?'

'Bless my barnacles,' replied Matthew, but showed no sign of wanting to leave.

Lizzie was at the tiller, which was unfortunate, as the area leader was trying to remove it for its nightly sojourn in the shed.

'Is this your little girl?'

Raymond acquiesced.

'Do you think you could move her? I've got to unfasten the tiller.'

'Why?'

'Because she might catch her fingers in it.'

'Why are you unfastening it?'

'We have to at half past four.'

'Oh, I see. I suppose the ship's on automatic pilot from now on.'

The girl made no attempt to smile. 'Vandals.' she said murkily.

'Come on you two.' He scooped up the vengeful Lizzie, who pummelled him angrily as he swung her over the side to the waiting buggy.

She ran away.

'Daddy.' Matthew was in the crow's nest.

'My goodness, you're high up. Come on down now, there's a good boy, and we'll go and get some tea.'

Matthew's face clouded. 'I can't.'

'Of course you can. Just come down the way you went up. Only the other way round.'

'I'm fwikened.'

On the way down Raymond tore his trousers on a nail on the mast.

After he had rescued Lizzie from the pinnacle upon which she was teetering, apparently prior to leaping on to a knotted rope some twenty feet away, he took them for tea in the wholefood café, where they consumed bran buns and flapjacks and Matthew spilt his prune juice.

On the way home he bought them Kitkats and delivered them to a sparkling Ginny at a quarter to seven.

She swept them up and bore them away, as Raymond hovered uncertainly in the untidy porch of his erstwhile home.

Ginny returned and asked, without looking at him, 'Have they got everything?'

'I think so.'

'Right.'

She closed the door.

As Matthew sat in the bath, she asked, 'Did you have a nice time?'

Matthew pondered the question, then nodded gravely.

'Excellent,' he said.

Helen hung up Raymond's coat and walked uncomfortably to the drinks cabinet.

'How was it?' she offered brightly.

Raymond considered for a moment.

'Excellent,' he said.

Mitchell sighed.

'You won't go, then?'

'Look, love, just because I work in a swimming pool doesn't mean my Mastermind subject's plumbing.'

'What is your Mastermind subject?'

'Anatomy.'

'Yours or mine?'

'Eileen's.'

There was a silence.

Ginny later remembered it as the only cruel remark he had ever made. She got out of bed and started to look for her sandals.

'I don't want to mess it up altogether. For aught I know about boilers, it'd blow up in her face the first time she turned it on.'

'Immersions.'

'You said boilers.'

'Immersions. It's the immersion.'

'You said it was the boiler.'

'Well, it doesn't really matter since you're not going to do it.'

'Ginny, I said I wouldn't do a boiler. An immersion's different. It's not the same thing.'

'Why not? They're both for hot water, aren't they?'

'So's a fucking kettle.'

'Don't swear at me.'

'I wasn't fucking swearing at you.'

'Why don't you go home?'

'Because I'm not welcome.'

'You're not welcome here either.'

Mitchell dressed himself quickly and went to the door.

Ginny was tidying a drawer in a fussy, unskilful way. He touched her shoulder but she didn't look up.

On the way out Mitchell noticed a pile of newspapers labelled '4th Acton Cub Scouts: To be collected' lying sodden by the path.

Raymond was looking for his car keys.

'Why don't you want to come?'

'I don't feel like it.'

'Why not?'

'I don't know. I just don't. I don't really like squash.'

'I thought you did.'

'Not really.'

Raymond stared at Helen suspiciously as he pulled on his coat. 'But you said how exciting it was the first time I took you.'

'Well, that's because. . .' Helen was thoroughly flustered. She's got a very low forehead, Raymond observed unfairly as Helen swept aside her non-existent fringe.

'Why do you do that?'

'Do what?'

'Keep dabbing at your hair like that. It's terribly irritating.'

Helen, who was quite unaware of her habit, gazed at him uncomprehendingly and repeated the gesture. Peevishness overwhelmed Raymond. 'There. You've done it again. Really, Helen, I don't think it's much to ask. . .'

'All right. I'll come.'

'You said you didn't want to.'

'Yes, I do. I've changed my mind.' She folded away the tapestry of two springer spaniels she had been working on and went into the bathroom.

'You don't have to, if you'd rather not.'

'I know. I'd like to. I'll just fix my make-up.'

Raymond listened to the clatter of rejected lotions followed by the sound of running water with mounting alarm. 'Are you going to be much longer? I'm meeting Des at seven thirty.'

'It's nearly that now.'

'Exactly. Are you ready?'

'Well, I've got to wash my hair.'

'You've what?'

'I can't go with my hair like this.'

'For Christ's sake, Helen, you won't be in the royal box.'

Helen appeared at the bathroom door, head covered in shampoo. 'If you want me to look a mess. . .'

'I don't care what you look like. I just want you to be ready.'

Helen's eyes were very moist. 'You should've told me earlier. I didn't want to come, anyway.'

'You just said you did.'

'Well, I've. . .'

'Changed your mind. Fine.' Raymond snatched up his squash kit and stamped out of the flat.

Once in the street he realised he'd forgotten the car keys so, unable to face the thought of another encounter with Helen, who, he knew from experience, would now be sobbing on the couch, he went in search of a taxi and was ten minutes late for his game.

'What about a drink?' Des asked after the customary thrashing.

Since the legendary encounter on Helen's first visit to the club, Raymond had, as yet, been unable to muster the form which had led to his spectacular victory. Des himself had read a warning in the defeat and had given up drinking lager beforehand. Consequently he drank a great deal afterwards, but although Raymond generally had a couple of pints to help him recover, he was usually speeding Wood Greenwards long before ten.

Tonight he stayed.

At first Des put his friend's moroseness down to a particularly bad defeat, but after a pint of beer and two whiskies it became clear that Raymond had more on his mind than the game of squash.

'What does Wendy do when you're playing?' he enquired.

'Oh, she's got a woodwork class. They usually go to the pub afterwards. She's in a worse state than me most evenings by the time she gets home.'

'Couldn't be as bad as Ginny,' Raymond declared. 'She only had to look at a bottle to start singing.'

'Ginny does like a drink,' Des agreed, 'but she's very funny when she's had a few.' Then, seeing Raymond's look of suffering, he changed to less dangerous topics. 'I may not be able to make it next week.'

'Why not?'

'Got to take the car in for a service. Wednesday's the only day they can manage.'

'Oh, right.'

'Do you want me to see if I can rustle up someone to give you a game?'

'No, that's all right. I probably won't bother. Helen doesn't like me playing every week.'

'She doesn't play herself?'

'No. Mind you, I don't like playing with women. They keep hurting themselves.'

'Oh, you mean Ginny and that friend of hers . . . Emily, was it?'

'Emma. Yes, the pair of them spent more time sticking plasters on than most people take for a match.'

'Everywhere, wasn't it? Elbows, ankles, racquets. . .'

'Yes, and remember that time Ginny knocked some poor bastard's glasses off and she insisted on mending them with the stuff?' Raymond shook with laughter. 'He looked such a berk with all that pink tape round his nose.'

'I think she did more damage to his dignity than his spectacles,' Des chuckled.

Raymond drained his glass. 'She certainly knows how to make people look small.'

The awful bitterness in his voice shocked Des. After all, wasn't it Raymond who had left Ginny? Raymond was the one with the brand-new love. 'Same again?' he asked to give his friend time to recover.

'Thanks,' said Raymond. 'Make it a double, could you?'

They sat for a while exchanging irrelevancies about the stock market and the latest test score, Raymond drinking his whisky with grim determination but no pleasure. The more he drank the clearer everything became.

'The thing is. . .' he kept saying, before turning once more to some item in that evening's *Standard*, or the number of projected job losses if BL was sold to General Motors. 'The thing is. . .'

The thing is, thought Des, he's cocked the whole thing up.

He looked at his watch. 'Come on. They're closing the bar. I'll give you a lift to the tube.'

Raymond lifted his head in surprise and seemed about to refuse. 'They're closing the bar,' Des repeated patiently. With a shrug Raymond picked up his jacket and fumbled for his bag under the chair.

Beyond lurching slightly as they made their way to the lift, his intoxication was unremarkable. Des drove him to Temple Bar and left him at the top of the steps. He would have offered to drive him all the way, but somehow he knew this was not the moment.

Raymond watched the rear lights of the car disappearing along the Embankment, then turned back to the station. He was halfway down the steps when, with awesome clarity, his brain flashed up the image of his projected homecoming: Helen, Victorian nightie and fluffy mules, face gleaming with vitamin E cream, hair washed, eyes worried, waiting for him. Always waiting. Waiting for him to choose the wine. Waiting for him to hold the door. Waiting for him to reach an orgasm. Waiting for him to go home. Slowly, methodically, he turned and made his way back up the steps and set off for the Green Room Club.

Raymond was very drunk. He leant lumpily against the hall door, carefully inspecting his keys.

Having tried three without success, he cursed roundly and launched himself at the bell.

A savage peal cut the night air, followed swiftly by the sound of Helen's mules cropping the Nairn.

'Where have you been? I thought something had happened to you.'

'It has.'

'I meant an accident.'

'I did try to throw myself under a train, but it seems I was in a taxi at the time. Sorry.'

He pushed past her and made his way to the drinks cupboard.

'Haven't you had enough?'

'As a matter of fact, I think I have.'

'Good, I'll make some coffee. Give me your coat.'

'I don't want any coffee. I want a drink. For God's sake, can't I have a drink in my own home? Not that this is my own home, is it, darling? It's my little love nest, where I stay with my little mistress, because I haven't got the guts to go back to my wife.'

Helen looked as though she'd been hit.

For a moment she stood, mouth slightly open, then, quite without warning, tears began to pour down her oval face.

Raymond observed her hazily, conscious that he had gone too far, but lacking the coherence to remedy it.

At last he sank down, head in hands, till he fell asleep. He awoke briefly in the small hours to be confronted by a mug of cold coffee at his elbow. Achingly he transferred himself to the couch and lay, crumpled and chilly, swaddled by raincoat, till daylight could no longer be ignored.

Helen left without breakfasting.

Once he almost encountered her sorrowful eyes flickering mournfully towards him, but he huddled deeper into his Burberry, and emitted snorting sounds like someone in a deep, if troubled, sleep.

Raymond got to the office at half past ten.

Maggie, his secretary, brought him a tray of coffee without

the cream jug, and when his baleful eyes met hers she stretched her lips reprovingly and returned to her typewriter.

The coffee cleared his head a little, and when Maggie
returned with some letters to be signed she found him
dictating gruffly into his Sanyo TRC 3500. As she turned
to go, a raucous grunt issued from her employer's larynx.
Raymond was clearing his throat.

Maggie recognised this as the official preamble to his
asking her opinion about something personal, so waited a
moment and then said, 'Did you want me to book your table
at L'Espagnole today, Mr Jeavons, or are you eating in?'

Raymond looked flustered. 'In, probably. That is, yes,
book it. No, don't. I'll, we'll . . . that is Helen and I. . . God,
Maggie, how can I eat with a head like this?'

'I'll leave it then, shall I? For now?'

'Yes, leave it. Thanks. . . Oh, Maggie. . .' to her retreating
form.

Maggie turned.

'Er, have you seen Helen this morning? I was a bit late
back last night – afraid I overslept, you know how it is?'

'Yes, I've seen her. Did you want me to get her?'

'No. No, don't do that. I just wondered, er, how she
looked.'

'She looked fine. A bit pale, I suppose, but then, she is
rather fair.' Maggie, whose loyalty to Raymond was beyond
question, could not bring herself to like the luckless Helen.

'Truth is, I had a few too many last night, and I'm rather
afraid I may have upset her – you know, said something
unfortunate. She looked all right, you say?'

'A bunch of flowers never comes amiss, Mr Jeavons. I
could order some if you like.'

'Could you do that, Maggie? I'd be awfully grateful.'

'And I'll book your table for one thirty, shall I?'

'Yes,' said Raymond cheerfully. 'Do that, would you?'

Helen, who had rigidly and properly refused promotion since
her liaison with Raymond had become public, was suitably

overwhelmed when a youth with lemon and lime pigtails stomped into the typing pool and roared, 'Any of you lot Helen Craig?'

'I am,' she confessed, turning pink.

'Here,' responded the boy graciously, and thrust an enormous bouquet of cellophane and tea roses into her unsuspecting arms.

The girls all cheered, and Helen retired to the Ladies to cry quietly before patching up her make-up and creeping timorously up to the third floor, where Raymond had his office.

'Who?' Ginny, who was painting her nails, tucked the phone under her chin and signalled to Matthew to turn the television down.

He turned it up.

'James? Oh, yes. How are you? Could you hold on a minute? . . . Matthew, turn it the other way . . . towards me. . . Not that one, the other one. . . That's right.'

'But now I can't hear it, Mummy.'

'Darling, I'm on the phone.'

'But I can't hear my programme if you're on the phone.'

'Sit closer to it.'

'I'll ruin my eyes.'

'Well, turn it off, then.'

Matthew did so and began to cry loudly at the injustice of the command. Lizzie tugged gently on the telephone cord till Ginny, whose chin muscles were unequal to the strain, dropped it with a resounding clang on the parquet floor. She managed to scoop it up before Lizzie got to it.

'James . . . are you still there?. . . Yes, sorry, I dropped it. . . It does rather, doesn't it? Still, better than a whistle.'

James, who was not entirely convinced of this, nursed his aching ear and tried again.

'I was just wondering if you're doing anything this evening?'

'Actually, yes,' lied Ginny. 'I've got to mend the washing machine.'

'What's the matter with it?'

'I don't know. I suspect sock-in-pump pox, but I won't know till I've baled it out.'

'It's just that Sally's gone down to her mother's for a couple of days with the kids, and I'm at a bit of a loose end. Wondered if you fancied a bite to eat and a glass of the old vino.'

Ginny grimaced. 'It's very kind of you, James, but honestly I've got to sort this machine out tonight. We're down to our last pair of pants.' Realising her mistake she added 'At least, Matthew is.'

James sighed. 'You had me going for a minute,' he spluttered. 'But look here, it won't take all night, will it? As the actress said to the archbishop.'

Ginny felt the irritation welling up in her, but fought on. 'To tell the truth, I'm a bit tired tonight. I've had a lousy cold and it's only just beginning to clear.'

'You sound all right to me.'

'Well, I'm not,' she snarled, with such vehemence that Matthew, who had been making an effigy with his fish fingers, looked up in joyful anticipation.

'Okay, Ginny,' James backed down. 'Another time, perhaps.'

'Yes,' Ginny softened, 'Another time.'

At a quarter past eight, as Ginny soaked blissfully in her Badedas, the doorbell rang. And rang. And rang.

On the fourth peal, fearful that Lizzie would wake and decide that one hour's sleep was as good as twelve, Ginny, swearing fiercely, struggled into her dressing gown and dripped down the stairs to the front door.

There stood James, bald and beaming, an array of paper carriers dangling from his podgy arms.

'I've got us a Chinese,' he informed her, 'and a bottle of you-know-what.' Ginny was so mesmerised by the absurdity

of the situation that she neglected to tell James what to do
with his you-know-what. Feebly she followed the prancing
accountant into the kitchen, where he strewed his banquet
across the remains of Matthew's jigsaw and several copies
of the *Radio Times*.

'Have a glass of this.' James handed her a tumbler of
Moroccan red. 'I think you'll like it.'

At a quarter past ten, having disposed of the red, and now
well into a ropey bottle of Trebbiano, Ginny ran out of
girlish banter, or rather, she ran out of replies to James's
facetious whimsicality.

She had known him for several years, but chiefly as an
associate of Raymond's and the husband of Sally, a pretty,
if innocuous, ex-school teacher, whose own conversation
centred mainly on the right age to stop breast-feeding. As
Ginny recalled, she had finally managed to wean her second
son on his third birthday, but whether she had ever been
able to dissuade her first from the practice remained a matter
for debate.

Now looking at James, she began to wonder if Sally's
manic devotion to the Breast is Best campaign was as innocent as she had hitherto supposed.

James's bobbly hand reached across the discarded foil
canisters. 'Come on, Ginny, you don't have to be shy with
me. We're old friends. . . Not so old, that is.' James swigged
copiously from the acid plonk. 'We all know things weren't
exactly hunky dory between you and Ray. No need to be
offended if I say you were wasted on him. . . No, don't say
a word. I know he's my friend – couldn't ask for a better – '

'I think he probably could,' interjected Ginny with
increasing irritation.

'But really, when you think about it, what sort of a guy
would walk out on his wife and kids for a bit of skirt half
his age?'

'When is Sally coming back?' snapped Ginny.

'What d'you say? Oh, Saturday. Catching the four o'clock.

Christ, that reminds me, I've got to order a guinea fowl. No, as I was saying, I've always been very fond of you, Ginny. I don't know what it is . . . it's not as though you're beautiful.'

'At least we have something in common.'

'No, I couldn't call you beautiful, but you've definitely got something. I can't put my finger on it.'

Ginny leapt sideways as James's hand struggled ineptly, but with surprising determination to undo her blouse.

'Then I wish to God you'd stop trying. Now, James, this has gone on quite long enough. It was very kind of you to buy me dinner, but now I want you to go home. I'm very tired and I've got a cold.'

'Ginny. . .' James lurched clumsily to his feet and flopped over her.

For someone so flabby, Ginny remembered thinking afterwards, he has incredibly strong hands.

'Oh, James, get off me. You'll catch my cold. Stop it at once. You're drunk.'

'You're adorable,' crooned James, who had had four whiskies before leaving home. 'You need a man, Ginny. That's what's missing from your life. A real man. I could be that man.' His hands slithered distractedly over her buttocks.

With a final exasperated wrench Ginny freed herself from the salivating swain. 'Let me know when you are,' she growled. 'Honestly, James. I've had enough. Go home at once.'

Again James's lips swooped, but Ginny was too quick for him.

As she slithered out of reach, James' mouth came into sharp contact with the light switch. He recoiled in pain.

'Now look what you've done,' scolded Ginny. 'You've hurt yourself. Stay there while I get a tissue.' Might just as well have said 'a Smartie', she thought, mopping the blood from James's petulant lip. Honestly, what a fuss! He's worse than Matthew. However does Sally put up with him?

'That could have been very nasty,' said James for the third time.

'My feeling exactly.'

'I hope there's no lead in that paint. A lot of these old houses are full of it.'

'I don't think even you could chip the paint with your lip, James.'

'Look there – by the switch – what's that, then?'

'That is where Raymond hit it with the side of the rocking horse. By mistake.'

James looked ready to dispute this, but Ginny had had enough, and shooed him into the hall, where she held his raincoat towards him, waiting patiently as he thrust his arms into the gaping sleeves and fumbled sulkily for his keys. His eyes were like pinheads as he rounded on his erstwhile hostess. 'You haven't got a cold,' he hissed. 'You're frigid.'

'Give my love to Sally and the children,' Ginny replied jauntily, and closing the door on him, she sank down on the carpet, helpless with giggles.

Thank God it's the last night, thought Ginny, preparing once more to buckle her Saxone cowboots for the showstopping 'The Farmer and the Cowman'.

That it would be a showstopper no one doubted, since it had effectively stopped the show every night that week. Three times due to the non-appearance of the cowman – who had a quick change and seemed incapable of buttoning his shirt and wearing his hat at the same time – and twice because of an electrical short which had plunged the pit in darkness, successfully eliminating both baton and score from the orchestral line of vision.

I wonder what it'll be tonight, mused Ginny. Please God, let the theatre catch fire before we start.

'Chorus for "The Farmer and the Cowman", please. This is your call for "The Farmer and the Cowman", ladies and gentlemen.'

Ginny trundled morosely down to the wings.

Laurie, a plain girl without eyebrows, was trying to be coy with Curly, who had the edge on her in this exercise. He dimpled and pouted while the young female trilled sadly at his crimped pate, occasionally stirring imaginary cowpats with her plimsolled foot.

' " People will say we're in love",' they crooned forlornly.

'People will say they're in B Flat,' snapped a falsetto cowpoke with a goatee beard who worked at the local branch of Laskys.

'Ssshh,' hissed Laurie's mother with a malevolence which branded her a hostile witness.

Roars of applause, whether from delighted relatives or relieved ratepayers, greeted the end of this duet.

The orchestra twanged uncertainly, striving to catch the glazed eye of Reggie, the conductor, to see if a fourth encore were required or whether they might still make the Lemon Tree before closing.

Naturally, they were out of luck.

Laurie and Curly circled each other grimly yet again and began to churn wanly through the last two verses.

This time the applause was noticeably muted, belying a universal desire for the performance to continue.

Thus it was that Ginny, wrapped in a gingham tepee and linked inextricably to a divorced optician, loped bitterly on to the boards of St Mark's Church Hall.

'Side together side front, dosey do and BOW', squeaked the goatee. 'Honour your partners. . .'

'Not again,' gasped Ginny, as the optician, who was clearly too wise to honour his own prescriptions, stepped neatly on to the bridge of her foot and retreated, beaming.

'I can't believe it's nearly over.' Ruby, a well-sprung soubrette who worked at Dolcis, teased her Oklahoma suntan nearer to Southall and replastered her azure lids. 'I shall be really miserable next week, I can tell you.'

Ginny concealed her disbelief as best she could.

She was saved from the need to reply by Marsha, who ran an aerobics class and wore myriad beaded plaits about her puffy face.

'What you worrying about, Ruby? Two weeks time we start on *West Side Story*. Better than this old rubbish.' She clicked invitingly. ' "I like to be in America. . ." '

' " OOOOklahoma. . ." ' retorted the tannoy, ' "Where the wind comes sweeping down the plain." '

'It's all right for you, Marsha. You'll get a good part. Not much for the likes of us in that, is there, Mrs Jeavons? It's all youngsters in that one.'

The lid of Ginny's thermos, which she had been coaxing to open, suddenly spun across the room like an Exocet. It broke.

'I dare say blacked up you might pass for fifty, Mrs Wetherall,' Ginny rasped and embarked on a purposeful exit which was only partially marred by her having forgotten to zip up her cowboots. Ruby stared after the limping traitress in mortified disbelief.

'Of course,' she confided to the world, 'we all know what's wrong with her.'

'How much longer, do you reckon?'

Ginny turned to see the shiny globe of Ronnie's face staring glumly from the prompt corner.

'Hullo. Shouldn't you be in the lighting box or somewhere?'

'Couldn't stand it any longer. There's four of them up there giving me advice. Jeesus. We've only got three lamps and one of them's bust. The other two are full up, so what else can I do? I says to them, "Look, mate, with what I've got here you're lucky you can see their bleedin' plimsolls!", pardon my French. "What d'you want?" I says to them. "Bleedin' flare paths?" I left 'em to it. How much longer d'you reckon?'

'This is the finale we've come down for. I suppose if we do five more encores, which is average, and allow for it being the last night, we should be through about nine o'clock tomorrow.'

'Christ, you think you're joking. Here, want some of this?'

'Oh, Ronnie, thanks. I don't think I'd better, though. You know what a lousy dancer I am, anyway.'

'Go on, it'll give you confidence. Bit of Dutch courage.'

'Oh, what the hell.'

Ginny was mildly aware that she was not in time with the others. This did not in itself dismay her since only by the greatest coincidence had she ever been. She was, however, also conscious of a rumbling amongst her fellow artistes – a flickering of sapphire lids askance, a furrowing of stencilled brows.

' "OOOOklahoma," ' they roared, ' "Where the wind comes right behind the rain." '

For some reason, this struck Ginny as funny, and, remembering Edward's exhortations for some hint of ebullience in this climactic sequence, she began to giggle.

The faces around her lengthened as the rib-cages swelled.

' "OOOOklahoma, Every night my honey lamb and I. . ." '

'OOOOklahoma,' Ginny echoed, a bar behind the rural cluster. 'Every night my spit-roast lamb and I, sit alone and talk, and watch the hawk shitting egg-sized pellets from the sky. . .'

No one spoke to Ginny.

A mawkish hush enclosed the dressing room. The thespians hissed in stifled tones more in keeping with a dentist's waiting room. Once or twice a discreet tap would draw a terracotta face to the door, where short, whispered interchanges would occur. These would engender further oblique glances to the spot where the culprit sat cheerily sponging her face. No one seemed quite able to relinquish the drama of the evening. They sat steadily on before their mirrors, unwilling to remove the first boot or prise away the first encrusted eyelash.

All except Ginny, who, scraping off a final trace of panstick, gazed joyfully at her scrubbed countenance, gathered her carriers around her and sprang doelike through their midst.

'Cheerio, everyone,' she crowed. 'Have a nice party.'

And went out into the corridor.

Where Raymond was waiting.

'But why did you throw your spear at that woman?' Raymond eyed her over his whisky. 'Surely it's not in the script?'

'It wasn't a spear. It was a hoe,' Ginny explained for the third time. 'I didn't throw it, anyway. I just lost my balance, and she happened to be in the way.'

'David might have said much the same about Goliath.'

'It was probably true in his case.'

'I grant you she wasn't very good, but a lot of the others were a damn sight worse. What about the one with the dustbin liner on his head?'

'Oh, Curly. Is that what it looks like from the front? I always wondered.'

'It looks as though he should be inside it.'

'Oh, come on, Raymond. Curly has a very nice singing voice.'

'How long have you been mixing with these people? Whose idea was it, anyhow?'

'Three guesses.'

'But Delia wasn't even there. Unless that was her in the taffeta loincloth.'

'She was backstage.'

'That accounts for a lot. What does she do? Wander around with someone else's head tucked underneath her arm?'

Ginny laughed. 'She did after Act IV. Honestly, it shows how unused to alcohol I am these days.'

'How much did you have?'

'Hardly any. Ronnie just gave me a few swigs while we were waiting to go on. Mind you, I don't think even he expected seven encores.'

'Who's Ronnie?'

'The electrician. They only put up with him because he can change plugs.'

'What's he like?'

'Oh, nothing much. Six foot three; green eyes; plays rugger. Why?'

'No reason. Just wondered if I might know him.'

'Shouldn't think so.'

'No. See much of him?'

'If you count double vision as much.'

'He's done it before, then?'

'What?'

'Got you drunk?'

'As a matter of fact, yes. At the dress rehearsal.'

'I'm surprised they let you go on. You could've jeopardised the entire proceedings.'

'You haven't changed at all, have you?'

'How do you mean?'

'You're still addressing me like the board of JCV.'

Raymond's worried eyes caught hers. 'I'm sorry. God knows, it's none of my business.'

'If it helps, Ronnie is five foot three tall and four foot nine wide, heavily married and eats garlic sausage. But he makes me laugh.'

Raymond glowed.

'As I say, it's none of my business. Does Matthew really miss me? I mean, he's never had much time for me in the past, has he?'

'That cuts both ways.'

'Is Lizzie driving you mad?'

'Faster than I'd thought.'

'I wish I could see them.'

'You do see them.'

Raymond's last defence had fallen. He stared at his wide, nobbly fingers and the signet ring which Helen had made him promise to wear.

'I don't see them in the bath,' he said. 'And asleep at night.'

Ginny gulped her Armagnac.

'You can look at them now.' she said. 'While I call you a cab.'

Raymond shut the door quietly. He stood for a moment, listening, before stealthily removing his overcoat and creeping into the living room. One lamp was still on, but there was no light from the bedroom, so he assumed Helen was asleep and poured himself a large whisky before sinking unhappily on to the couch.

He sat for some time thinking about the night's events – Ginny's appalling behaviour. Why did he still feel responsible for her? Why was he pleased the electrician was fat? What did it matter if she attacked strange women in tablecloths, particularly in full view of four hundred people? She was obviously mad. Perhaps he could have her certified and get custody of the children. . .

Matthew still snored. Lizzie, cherubic against the sheets. . . Did she even know who he was anymore?

Did he want them without Ginny?

What would Helen say?

'Where have you been?'

'Eh?'

Raymond swung round as a wide-eyed Helen in a Laura Ashley negligée closed in on him.

'Where have you been? I've been sick with worry.'

'I had to see someone.'

'You could have phoned.'

'I tried to. The line was engaged.'

'When?'

'I don't know. Seven o'clock. About.'

'Who did you have to see?'

'No one you know. Mallingham. He's a rep. I didn't think it would go on so long. I'm sorry.'

'It is Saturday.'

'I know. I do apologise. I should have phoned again, but it was tonight or tomorrow, so I thought, rather than mess up a Sunday. . .'

'It's your Sunday for the children.'

'Yes.'

'So if it's a matter of them or me. . .'

'You know that's not true.'

'It is true. I come second. I always have.'

'Helen, I only see them once a fortnight. I see you every day.'

'I bet you wish it was the other way round.'

And so it went on – recriminations, denials, accusations, tears. . .

As Raymond finally bedded down for another night on the sofa his head swam with the sound of Helen's strictures.

What did she expect? What did she want from him?

Of course his children came first. How long before he said as much? How long before he stopped protesting his undying love for her? How long before he stopped pretending?

How long before he spoke to her the way he spoke to Ginny?

Eileen sat down.

Flanked by a mass of quilted poncho from which only a runny nose protruded, and a diminutive oriental who appeared on the brink of dissolving, she felt claustrophobic and miserable. Reaching for a magazine, she knocked over her bag and scrambled after the contents, which no one seemed inclined to help her rescue. Furtively she retrieved the small polythene bag and shrank back against the padded bench, her head deep in the pages of *Woman's Weekly*.

'Do You Really Need Sex?' The accusing face of the journal's pet GP stared angrily up at her.

Hurrying on, she was assaulted by a twelve-page supplement of cream recipes. It was called 'Naughty, but Nice.'

'Mrs Mitchell.'

Eileen shot to her feet, clasping her bag ferociously.

The nurse smiled conspiratorially. 'Would you go through to Dr Randall, please. On the left.' Eileen crept along the corridor, convinced of the patients' muffled whispers behind her.

'Good morning, Mrs Mitchell. What seems to be the problem?'

Eileen stared incredulously at the doctor.

'Aren't you feeling well?' he enquired.

'No. Well, yeah. That is, I think I'm pregnant.'

'Splendid. That's just what you wanted, isn't it? Is your husband pleased? I'm sure he is. I take it that you want confirmation. What I'll need is a small sample. . .'

'I've got it.' Eileen fumbled frantically and produced the polythene bag, extracting from it a small bottle marked Witch Hazel. 'Is that enough?' she quavered. 'Only I can do another if you want.'

'That will be fine, Mrs Mitchell. Is it this morning's?'

'Ten past six. Is that all right?'

'I'm sure it will be. I'll have it sent off, and we should know for sure by the end of the week.'

'The end of the week?' Eileen gazed at him, appalled. 'I thought you could do it now.'

'I'm afraid not. You see, all our samples have to go to Hammersmith for analysis. We haven't the facilities here. You'll find the time will pass quite quickly. Now, I need a few details. When was your last period?'

'Last month.'

'Can you remember the dates?'

'September the fifth.'

'So you've just missed one so far?'

'That's enough, isn't it?'

'Usually, yes. Some people are irregular.'

'I'm not.'

'Right. How are you feeling?'

'Sick.'

'That's certainly another indication. I would advise you to avoid any form of medication at this time. You may find a dry biscuit beside your bed will help to settle you before you get up in the morning. That often does the trick. Get your husband to bring you a cup of tea. Don't rush to get going. Now you give my receptionist a call on Friday, after eleven, and I hope we'll have some good news for you.'

Eileen slunk into the street. Four days. What should she do? She could get it done at the chemist, but that was six quid, and anyway she knew. What difference did it make whether it was official?

She had to tell Mitchell before he guessed. So far she'd only been sick twice. He thought she'd picked up a virus and told her to stay in bed till he got home. But she couldn't do that. She had to find Gerry.

'Mummy,' Matthew's face presaged a disaster.

'Yes, darling?'

'I have sad news for you.'

'Oh dear. What is it?'

'You will never be a 'lympic champion.'

'That is sad,' his mother agreed. 'But I think you're probably right.'

'I am right,' Matthew affirmed with authority and returned to his camp – an ingenious construction of bedding, bin liners and most of what Ginny needed to clean the house.

'Are you having lunch in there, or do you want to watch "Rainbow"?' Ginny was rather hoping Matthew would opt for the latter, which would allow her to repossess the ironing board, albeit temporarily.

'Too much television is bad for my eyes.'

'I don't suppose it's any worse for them than sitting under a blanket all day.'

She was beginning to regret having allowed him to spend a weekend at Rosie's. Since his return a constant flow of platitudes had dripped from his lips, eroding what little patience she could muster these days.

'I want my lunch in my camp.'

'What do you say?'

'Pleeeease.'

'Well, say it.'

'I did say it.'

'Not till I told you to.'

'Do what I say, not what I do,' came the muffled response.

Ginny snarled and turned to the two fish fingers blackening silently under the grill. 'Do you want ketchup with your lunch?'

'What am I having?'

'Fish fingers.'

'Some people can swim like fishes.'

'No doubt.'

'You can't, can you, Mummy?'

'No, Matthew, there are a lot of things I can't do like a fish.'

'Bet you wish you could.'

Ginny pondered the suggestion, but lacked enthusiasm for it. 'Not really.'

'Why not?'

'I don't like getting wet.'

'*I* don't like getting wet.'

'Snap.'

'I'm not having a bath tonight.'

'Oh, don't start that. Come on, eat your lunch.'

'Some people have fishes on their feet.'

The charred morsels slithered on to his trainers as Matthew upended his plate. 'Well, you have now. I do wish you'd watch what you're doing.' The child scooped up his lunch and withdrew once more into the folds of his den.

There was silence for a moment as Matthew hid the unwanted meal.

'They have them all the time.'

'Who have what?'

'People have fishes.'

'On their feet?'

'They don't have proper feet, they just have fishes.'

'Oh, mermaids. Yes, that's right.'

'How do they walk?'

'They don't. They just sit about on rocks, combing their hair.'

'Like Aunty Vicky?'

Ginny choked on her Ryvita. 'Yes, Matthew. Just like Aunty Vicky.'

'Where do they live?'

'They live at the bottom of the sea. They've got a king called Neptune who's in charge of them all.'

'Do they hold their noses?'

'I expect they get used to the smell after a while.'

'Not the smell. The water. How can they breathe in the water?'

'Oh, mermaids are magic. They're not like us. Mermaids can breathe.'

'Is Mr Mitchell a mermaid?'

'Not that I've noticed.'

'He can swim a whole length under the water.'

'Yes, but he hasn't got fish on his feet.'

'He might grow some.'

'We shall have to keep an eye on him.'

'Yes,' Matthew assented. 'Can I watch "Rainbow"?'

'Oh, hallo, Eileen.' Susan looked slightly pink.

'Hallo, Sue. D'you think I could come in for a minute?'

'Course. Thing is, I was on my way to the depot, and I'm a bit late.' She hovered apologetically in the doorway.

'It won't take a minute. I need to ask you something.' Eileen stood like an unsuccessful sales rep, assured of defeat but destined to meet it head-on.

'Okay, then. Just for a mo.'

Still grasping the now innocent bag, Eileen began, 'I was wondering if you've seen anything of Gerry lately?'

Susan fiddled with her make-up. 'Not for a while. Not since we all went to that club with Jimmy and Jackie. When was that? Must be about three weeks.' 'It's longer than that,' said Eileen. 'That was the last time I saw him. It's six weeks ago.'

'Was it really?' The slits widened. 'I didn't think it was that long. Still, I suppose it must've been.'

'I thought he might've been round here.'

'No, not that I remember. Mind you, I'm not always in. Mam might know. She's out just now. I could ask her if you like.'

'No,' said Eileen hopelessly. 'No, don't. You don't know where I could get hold of him, do you?'

'Well, the truth is, Eileen, I think he's gone back to camp. I mean, I think his leave's over now.'

'Have you got his address?'

Susan recognised her mistake. 'Mind you, I'm not sure. Come to think of it, I think he was going down to Cardiff to see a mate of his for a while before he went back. Yes, I think that's where he is, so perhaps he'll pop in before he goes back. Shall I tell him you called?'

Eileen kissed her last chance goodbye.

'Yes, please,' she murmured, and turned to go.

'How's that lovely hunk of a husband of yours?' Susan called brightly.

But Eileen didn't answer.

'This is very nice of you, Mr Mitchell,' Alice called into the depths of the airing cupboard, where Mitchell lay surrounded by wire and table napkins. 'I'm just making a cup of tea, if you'd like one.'

'Ank oo urry uch,' he managed through the mouthful of nails. On emerging some twenty minutes later, he found Alice in the kitchen engrossed in the *Radio Times*.

She rose as he came in, and moved to the kettle.

'Would you prefer tea or coffee?'

'Tea please. That should do you all right now. The cable was frayed. It kept cutting out. I've put a new bit in. Should be all right.'

'I can't tell you how grateful I am. It's been driving me mad, never knowing whether I can have a hot bath or not. I do love my bath, don't you?'

'It's very nice,' said Mitchell.

'Would you like a chocolate Penguin?' Seeing him demur, she added, 'I'm going to have one,' and fetched a small tin from the larder. 'I buy them for my grandson, but I'm afraid I always finish them up between visits. He's only allowed two, you see, and there are six in a packet. Blue or red?'

'Blue please.'

'I expect you know Matthew and Lizzie, if you're a friend of Ginny's?'

'Yes,' agreed Mitchell. 'I used to have the lad for swimming. That's where we met.'

'I'm very fond of Matthew, and Lizzie, although she's a frightful handful these days. Do you know, last time she was here we were all watching *Spartacus*, and as you'll remember, it's a very long film. I love Kirk Douglas, don't you? Anyway, Lizzie got bored. She turned the set off twice, so Ginny put her out of the room, but of course she came back in and the next thing we heard was this frightful rumbling sound. I thought the washing machine was on the blink, but sure enough, it was Lizzie. Would you believe, that child pushed a Victorian spoonback chair right across the sitting room and shoved it in front of the television so none of us could see a thing. Then she sat in it so we all had to look at her. I must say she does make me laugh, though. Have you got any children, Mr Mitchell?'

'No, we haven't.'

'Still, you're young yet, aren't you? And they are a frightful handful. I suppose it's all right if you get nice ones like Matthew and Lizzie, but my two often made me wonder if it was really worth it. Still do, if it comes to that. More tea?'

Mitchell laughed.

'Surely they're off your hands by now?'

'You'd be amazed. Eric's all right, I suppose, but he does whine so. And Raymond. . . Mind you, I think she's probably better off without him. He was getting so pompous, and, of course, Ginny hates anything like that. I shouldn't be going on like this. I don't know what's got into me. The prospect of a long hot bath, I expect. I feel quite heady. Of course, I left my husband when the boys were young. Older than Ginny's two, but not much. It wasn't the thing to do in those days, either. There was a great deal of ill-feeling on both sides of the family about it, I remember. I can't help wondering if some of it didn't rub off on them. They didn't seem much bothered at the time, but you never really know, do you? I think Matthew misses his daddy dreadfully. Do you want another biscuit? I've got some digestives.' Mitchell stood up.

'No, thanks. I must be going. As I say, you should be all right now. Let Ginny know if it cracks up again and I'll take another look.'

'I'm sure it will be fine. I have every confidence in you, Mr Mitchell.'

Mitchell grimaced, remembering how Ginny had warned him of Alice's obsession with the nobility of British artisans.

'Now, how much do I owe you?'

'Nothing.'

'Oh, really, Mr Mitchell, I can't possibly let you do it for nothing.'

'I've had a chocolate Penguin.'

'I wish the Gas Board was so accommodating. Are you really sure?'

'Certainly, I'm sure. I'm a friend of Ginny's.'

Alice, watching him drive away, suddenly understood which friend he was.

Helen had a spot.

She'd noticed that since she'd been back on the pill her skin was no longer quite so immaculate, particularly round her chin.

She gazed at her face with loathing. Eyes still bright with tears, nose gleaming from the brute force of two hours' non-stop blowing, hair lank and shapeless from anguished twisting. And now: a spot.

No wonder he doesn't want me, she pondered miserably. Nobody would want me. I'm stupid and immature, my puddings have Sweetex in, and now I've got spots!

She laid her pounding head on her lissom arms and began to wail anew. After a while she found that they ached and that she had pins and needles in her left hand, so she raised her head and dragged herself forlornly to the basin to rinse her face.

Raymond's shaving mirror challenged her from above the taps. Masochism prevailed and she gazed in morbid fascination at the red and yellow circles of her magnified blemish, then leant forward purposefully and squeezed it sharply between the nails of her thumb and forefinger. An angry crimson sprang into the blotch but it did not burst. Helen ran the hot tap till it scalded her, and slapped boiling cotton wool on to the offending spot till her eyes streamed and her nose retracted.

It glowed back at her, unvanquished.

Cursing, she fumbled through her make-up bag until, with a sob of triumph, she pulled out her tweezers and, with the precision of a surgeon and the ecstacy of a torturer, whipped off the protective crust. A solitary drop of blood surged to the surface. Helen dashed it away in a sea of TCP, and stood back, victorious.

'This won't do,' she declared implacably. 'I can do better than this,' and she began to wash her hair.

Raymond knew as he left the flat that morning that he would not be going back.

How could he?

The things he had said to Helen last night came flooding back with the kind of recall he had hoped was reserved for Judgement Day. 'Immature', 'naïve', 'inexperienced' – his accusations came crashing through his consciousness as he walked unsteadily to the tube. And what about his children? She resented them; that was obvious. Tried to stop him seeing them.

When had she ever done that before? She was marvellous about his weekend visits. Encouraged him, cheered him up when he came back, cooked him delicious dinners, even if she did put sweeteners in the dessert. Good God, had he really mentioned the puddings? The word 'Sweetex' echoed round his beleaguered brain like the bells in the Irving melodrama. How could he have been so crass, so insensitive, so . . . drunk? What could he do? Helen would never have him back again.

Or perhaps she would.

Which would be worse? Yet another reunion courtesy of Moët and Interflora, or finding himself out on the streets of Wood Green with no one to iron his shirts for him?

Each reconciliation became harder to effect. It was all so contrived: saying he didn't know what had come over him. She was all he really cared about. Without her he was nothing. A nobody . . . Christ, the lies were worse than the arguments.

What was he doing it for? How long could they possibly go on this way? Where could he go if he *did* leave her? What would she do if he did? Why couldn't she meet someone else? What, in God's name, was so special about him?

Raymond left the station and made his way to Green Park. He walked slowly round it once, then round it again quickly.

He arrived at his office shortly before noon, bright with decision.

As the building gradually emptied for lunch he made his way to Roebuck's empty office.

He would phone Ginny. Then he would order the tea roses.

'Why are you ringing me up?' Ginny doodled violently over the telephone bill.

There was a silence, then Raymond cleared his throat again.

'Ginny. There's something I'd like to talk to you about.'

Ginny waited. The doodle was assuming the vigour of a brass-rubbing.

'Could you. . . Do you think. . . For Christ's sake, Ginny, can we have lunch together?'

'So long as I don't have to cook it.'

'No, of course not. We could go to a restaurant.'

'Or the JCV canteen.'

'Why there?'

'We always go there. Or we did.'

Raymond decided to give up. What was he doing, skulking in someone else's office in the lunch hour, asking favours of the world's number one bitch, when he had a young, sensual mistress itching for him in Wood Green?

'Where would you like to go?'

'Le Gavroche.'

'Seriously.'

'I'm perfectly serious.'

'I can't afford it.'

'We could go Dutch.'

'I still can't afford it.'

'What about Hosteria Romana?'

'I can afford that.'

'Is Helen coming?'

'What's all this?' Raymond looked mildly embarrassed as he was confronted by the candles glistening over the avocados *Aurora*, the filigree brown bread and the Meursault lapped by ice cubes. 'Is it my birthday?'

'Your birthday's in June,' Helen admonished. 'It's our anniversary.'

Raymond swallowed nervously.

'Four months and one week.'

'I'm awful about that sort of thing. Ginny always used to say. . .' his voice petered out. 'My God, Helen, this is a '76. You really are becoming a wine buff.'

Helen put her hands on his shoulders. 'With you to teach me, there's nothing I can't learn.' She kissed him softly on the mouth and moved away. She smelled wonderful.

The beef Wellington was worth a Michelin star, the parsleyed potatoes crumbled delicately in his mouth, the raspberry sorbet betrayed no hint of saccharin.

Helen brought him his Armagnac on the couch and nestled down between his thighs, one hand resting lightly on his knee.

Her skin glowed translucent in the lamplight.

Raymond reflected dreamily what a superb creature she was.

As she led him, siren-like, to the bedroom, neither of them noticed the discarded contraceptives lying in the pierrot wastebasket.

The clinic was suffocating.

Wet emulsion pervaded the already fetid atmosphere, adding significantly to the waves of nausea which swept over Eileen in this, her tenth, week of pregnancy.

She found a gap between two cone-shaped women, whose

spreadeagled thighs lapped over her tightly clenched knees, forcing her to compress herself still more.

I'm going to be sick, she thought resentfully, trying to summon the will to struggle once more to the farthingaled triangle across the room.

'Mrs Hetherington, Mrs Porter, Mrs Nazuki, Mrs Leather, Mrs Blanch.'

Eileen's bookends prised themselves away from the vinyl bench and waddled after the nurse.

The room seemed suddenly larger.

Eileen lent forward and grasped a handful of *My Weekly*'s. More cream recipes and a eulogy to syrup. Egg yolks also featured heavily.

When she returned from the lavatories her place had been taken. A thin fair woman with navy rings beneath her eyes, about Eileen's age, was slumped where she had been. Eileen sat down next to her, feeling better and almost sorry for the well-dressed girl who looked so ill and awful.

Thank God I don't look like that, thought Eileen. He'd leave me if I was that ugly. But of course she knew he wouldn't. Not just for being ugly. There'd have to be something else. Anyway, he's pleased. He's so happy. What can I do? Poor sod. Pray it doesn't have black hair.

The fair girl was trying to read a paperback. *Far From The Madding Crowd*, Eileen deciphered laboriously. She'd seen the film, so felt a tinge of superiority, since she knew how it would end.

She noticed that the girl didn't turn over any pages. Still, there weren't any pictures so it probably took a while. Eileen didn't like reading. She couldn't see the sense in it.

'Mrs Foster, Mrs McClintock, Mrs Mitchell, Mrs French, Mrs Jeavons.' The girl started guiltily at this last name, as though she would prefer not to admit to it. Eileen felt a twinge of curiosity, but she had problems of her own.

They filtered through with their urine and returned with their leaflets.

'Thank you,' said Ginny, after she had kissed him.

'I haven't done anything yet.'

'The immersion.'

'Oh, yes. It was no bother.'

'What was wrong with it?'

'Frayed connections.'

'Sounds like a pop group.'

Mitchell couldn't think of a reply, so said nothing.

'How was Alice?'

'Who?'

'Alice. My mother-in-law.'

'She looked fine. For someone who hadn't had a bath for two hours.'

'Well, you know how old people are.'

'Not really. Although I must say, she didn't seem like an old person to me.'

'No?'

'No. More like a calmed-down version of you.'

'You can't get calmer than me. I'm so calm, I flow.'

'Who told you that?'

'No one. I'm learning yoga. I am at peace with myself and the world. For at least thirty seconds a day.'

'When's the lucky day?'

'I believe I've taught you cynicism.'

'You've taught me the Singapore Grip.'

'The nearest East you'll get is Eileen of New Cross.'

'Why do you want a row?'

'I've had bad news.'

'Who from?'

'Raymond.'

He waited.

'It seems he wants to come back.'

'How do you know?'

'He told me.'

'Just like that?'

Ginny shrugged. 'We had lunch last Thursday.'

'And?'

'He says it was all a mistake. He never wanted to leave. He was pushed into it, " manoeuvred". Helen is too young, "too adolescent", doesn't understand the first thing about him. He misses the children. His work is suffering. He's worried about Alice, his job, *my* health, will you note. Need I say more?'

Mitchell leant against the bedhead.

'When's he coming?'

'I don't know. I've said he must sort it out with Helen. Poor girl. It's bound to be a shock. She'll get over it, of course. You always do. But it does hurt. Whatever people say.'

'Are you glad?'

Ginny looked at Mitchell's glorious face. 'Of course I'm glad. I'm glad because I have two children who need a father, because I'll have to drink less and eat more, because bald, fat middle-aged zombies will stop treating me like a tart, and most of all I'm glad because now I'll have to stop thinking about you day and night and learn to be suburban again.'

And Ginny leant over and cried till she was ugly, and Mitchell thought he probably loved her, now it was over.

'This is marvellous news.' Delia's cup struck the saucer like a cymbal. 'I'm delighted. Richard will be too. Well done.'

'I haven't actually done anything.'

'Nonsense. I told you it would be all right. What a good thing you took my advice. Because I have to tell you frankly, Ginny, sometimes you can be a little pig-headed.'

Ginny refrained from enquiring which of Delia's many magic words had done the trick. Delia would have taken credit for the Wooden Horse after two viewings of *Zorba The Greek*.

'When's he coming? Are the children excited? How's Matthew these days? Still. . .'

'Thin,' Ginny finished. 'Yes, he is rather.'

'Oh dear,' sighed Delia. 'Still, perhaps when Daddy's back he'll find his appetite. They do miss them, you know. You don't realise it at the time, but years later it comes out. Look at the courts. Full of children from broken homes.'

'Fortunately, Matthew's not yet legally culpable.'

'I don't think Matthew will be your main problem,' Delia conceded, as she prised Lizzie's talons from her support hose. 'Oh, really, Ginny, what have you been feeding this child? She's covered me in syrup.'

'It was a bit of roly-poly', said Ginny. 'I don't want her to be thin like Matthew.'

'Well, if you ask me, the sooner they get a bit of parental discipline the better. I know it hasn't been easy for you, Ginny, but you must admit they've got a bit out of hand.'

For the only time in her life, Ginny looked Delia full in the face.

'In what way?'

'Oh, you know very well. Let's not pretend everything's been hunky-dory. Raymond may have been at fault. He certainly was, but you haven't exactly pined away waiting for him, have you?'

'No,' said Ginny, 'I haven't. And if you need any more slime for the *Mothers' Trust News*, why not tell them that the blessed Ginny Jeavons, whose magnanimous spouse is deigning to return, now that he knows his teenaged temptress can't suck cock, is not exactly over the moon at the prospect.'

'Be that as it may,' sniffed Delia. 'I'd better be off. Sometimes I wonder if you know who your real friends are. What you could see in Ronnie Clarkson I'll never know. And you know, he is a married man.'

'Most men are,' said Ginny, mainly to herself.

'You won't forget the meeting on Thursday?' called Delia, as she revved up.

'No,' said Ginny. 'Of course not.'

Matthew grasped Alice's arm as she trundled the buggy back up the hill.

'Shall I tell you a secret, Grammar?'

'Yes, please.'

'You mustn't tell anyone, will you?'

'No, of course not.'

'Daddy's coming home.'

'Oh, that's nice. When?'

'I don't know.'

'Are you glad?'

'Not very. I am a bit.'

'I'm sure you are really.'

'No.'

'Why not?'

'I'll have to go to bed early.'

'Is that the only reason?'

'Yes.'

'Think of all the nice things. You'll be able to play football and go swimming with him.'

'I play football with Mummy. And go swimming.'

Alice cursed herself but still said, 'Who do you go swimming with?'

Matthew marvelled at her ignorance. 'With Darren, of course.'

'Who's Darren?'

'Darren. He's in my class.'

'Haven't you missed Daddy a little bit?'

'No.'

'I expect you have. It's been hard for Mummy, taking care of you and Lizzie all by herself.'

'She didn't.'

'Yes she did.'

'She didn't. She had people to help her.'

'People aren't the same as Daddy.'

'Mr Mitchell is.'

Raymond sat with Des, in the bar of the Ploughman's Arms.

'How did she take it?'

Des, a basically uxorious man with a teenaged daughter, was torn between a wish to see his friend's marriage restored and the memory of his offspring's suicidal misery when her student boyfriend departed for an archaeological dig in Haifa on the arm of a female disc jockey from Peterborough.

Raymond, grey from lack of sleep, shook his head slowly.

'She cried. Of course I knew she'd cry. Thought she would, anyway. She didn't really cry all that much. Kept asking me what she'd done wrong.

'I told her it wasn't anything she'd done or hadn't done. Over and over again I told her. I don't think she was listening. I said it was my fault. She'd be better off without me. All that. I wanted to leave tonight, but she was in such a state. Made me promise to stay till Saturday. Said it was all she would ever ask me. That I could go after that and she'd never say another word.

'Poor girl. I think she was hysterical, but what could I do?'

'Where is she now?'

'In bed. Looked terrible, poor thing. It must have been the shock, I suppose. It affects some people like that.'

'Wears them out?'

'That too, of course, but Helen wasn't at all well. In fact, she was sick. Awfully sick.'

Ginny wished it hadn't been a pub. A bus station would have seemed more personal than the vaulted mahogany ceilings of the cavernous saloon. The sight of beef pasties drying in the microwave and the raucous chunter of lunchtime customers enjoying themselves struck her as unusually callous on this particular Friday.

They sat side by side on a mock Victorian pew, pretending it didn't matter.

'Are you glad?' Mitchell asked again, out of nothing.

This time Ginny said nothing. Her mouth was dry, like someone at the dentist. If she pulled the cotton wool out, would it feel all right again?

Mitchell squeezed her hand.

'I think it's for the best, really.'

Ginny looked at him.

'You see, there's something I've been wanting to tell you.'

'Officer,' she interjected.

Mitchell smiled. 'Finish your drink,' he said.

'My darling, unless you are about to tell me that you, or worse still I, have a terminal illness, I'd prefer not to be blind drunk when I hear it.'

'Eileen's pregnant.'

Ginny finished her drink. 'That's nice.'

Mitchell sat for a moment, quiet.

'Yes,' he said at last.

Ginny gazed at him. Shyly she touched his arm.

'It's what she wanted,' she said. 'It's what you both wanted, really. You may not think so, but it is. And you are right. It is for the best.'

'Yes,' said Mitchell again. 'Only thing is, it's not mine.'

Ginny went to the bar. When she returned, she asked, 'How do you know?'

Mitchell shrugged. 'What does it matter. I know.'

'What will you do?'

'Nothing.'

'You must. You'll wreck your marriage if you don't. You'll ruin the child's life.'

'You don't understand,' he said slowly. 'It doesn't matter whose it is. Eileen's my wife. She wanted a baby and she thought I couldn't give her one. For all I know it is mine.'

Ginny paused, then said, 'It probably is. If you think about it, it's bound to be.'

Mitchell rubbed his finger round the top of his glass.

'The thing is, even if it *is* mine, Eileen will always think it isn't. And she'll never be able to tell me.'

Ginny sipped the vodka, but she didn't want it.

Mitchell stood up. He seemed undecided what to do next.

'Will I see you? At the pool?' he asked.

'I don't think so' she said. 'Matthew's suddenly developed an interest in judo. Of all things.'

Mitchell nodded and half smiled at her, then he turned and walked sadly away.

He didn't hear as Ginny, for the first time in her life, said softly, 'Goodbye, David.'

Ginny picked up the phone.

'Oh, hallo, Raymond. What is it?'

Raymond felt Helen's adoring arms round his disappearing waist.

'Ginny, I'm afraid I've got something to tell you. . . It's about Helen. . .'

He told her.

'Who was that?'

'Daddy.'

'When's he coming? Are we going to meet him? Has he brought us a present?'

Ginny looked at Matthew's jubilant moon of a face and thought, on the whole, she'd rather drown.